Oliver Grey

The rhymes and rhapsodies of Oliver Grey

Oliver Grey

The rhymes and rhapsodies of Oliver Grey

ISBN/EAN: 9783337270650

Printed in Europe, USA, Canada, Australia, Japan

Cover: Foto ©Andreas Hilbeck / pixelio.de

More available books at **www.hansebooks.com**

THE

RHYMES AND RHAPSODIES

OF

OLIVER GREY.

LONDON and NEW YORK:

GEORGE ROUTLEDGE & SONS, LIMITED.

1898.

TO CYNTHIA.

La belle rose du printemps
Aubert, admoneste les hommes
Passer joyeusement le temps
Et pendant que jeunes nous sommes
Esbattre la fleur de nos ans.

PIERRE DE RONSARD.

DEAR Muse,
    Whom I have wooed
  In many a mood,
Gathering flowers
Of happy hours;
To thy fair use
  A wreath I bind
  Of eglantine.

What though
  My song be slight,
  And numbers light
As gossamer,
And I incur
Men's blame, I trow
  Thy favour kind
  May yet be mine.

So, here,
  Even at thy feet,
  My Lady sweet,
These rhymes I lay,
And fondly pray
The gift sincere
  May welcome find
  Upon thy shrine.

CONTENTS.

RHYMES AND RHAPSODIES.

NEW YEAR'S EVE.

THREE minutes to twelve ! and the Year
    Has only three minutes to live.
Ah ! what would we give,
      If the tear,
That springs to our eyes
      As he dies,
Could recall us the life, loved so dear.

Two minutes to twelve !   How the past
    With its laughter, its sighs, and its pain
    Crowds fast through the brain !
      Stay your flight !
Hearken, Year, to our prayer
      Of despair,
Ere your last breath fades out on the night.

One minute to twelve! To my heart
Cling closer, my Sweet. Let the Year,
On the threshold that 's near,
Find us true,
While together we stand,
Hand in hand,
And I watch by the window with you.

Twelve o'clock ! Kiss me, Sweet, for the past,
And again for the time that shall be.
What it brings you and me,
Who can say ?
Little matter, so long
As no wrong
Steal our love for each other away.

'T IS WINTER YET.

Là du plaisant Avril la saison immortelle
Sans eschange le suit
La terre sans labeur, de sa grasse mamelle
Tout chose y produit.
                                        RONSARD.

I know a time shall be,
    When from each slumbering bough
Shall flash on you and me
    The beautiful young leaves,
        Like glimmering emeralds set
        In April's coronet :
When the warm south wind shall sough,
    And to the silent eaves
        The twittering martlets cling,
        With tidings of the spring.
            Ah, me ! 't is winter yet.

I know a time shall be,
    When, for our sweet delight,
The pretty pageantry
    Of April shall unfold ;
        The herald violet,
        With purple banneret ;
Gay kingcups bravely dight
    In shining cloth of gold ;

And, dancing in the breeze,
Virgin anemones.
Ah, me! 't is winter yet.

I know a time shall be,
When on my longing ear
Your voice, a melody
Of silver strings, shall sound,
And charm away the fret
Your absence doth beget ;
When Love shall cast out Fear
In chains eternal bound,
And, coming to his own,
Raise in our hearts his throne.
Ah, me! 't is winter yet.

I know a time shall be,
When all save Love shall fail ;
That dim futurity
When we, dear Heart, must stand
Where life and death are met.
May there be no regret,
As, down the stream, we sail
Toward the shadowy land
Where, crowned with asphodels,
Spring time for ever dwells.
Ah, me! 't is winter yet.

DE PROFUNDIS.

THE waves break ceaseless o'er the bar,
   And, creeping softly to the land,
      Fall desolate.
Above, a solitary star
   Pierces the gloom.   Alone I stand
Before the great,
     The limitless Unknown,
     Like driftwood thrown
   Upon the eternal strand;
An atomy forlorn of Fate.

Yet have I comfort in distress;
   For, even as the star that gleams
      Across the night
Pilots the sailor to the ness,
   So, with the solace of her beams,
Faith, burning bright,
     Points me the goal,
     O'er reef, by shoal,
   To that dear land of dreams,
Where bloom the flowers of heart's delight.

MELANCHOLY.

A MONG the balmy willow buds,
   The bees are murmuring low ;
Bird music all the welkin floods ;
   The spring winds come and go.
Only my heart is sad to-day :
Sweet April, charm my grief away.

The butterfly, on satin wings,
   Pursues his bridal quest ;
And loud the minstrel blackbird sings
   His Love upon her nest :
Spring, that makes every creature glad,
Why should my heart alone be sad ?

ANIMA, VAGULA, BLANDULA.

SPRING, and the sunset:
    Cloudless, azure days:
The hills in haze:
Peace everywhere.
Only the heart
Cries, in the sunny noon,
"Spring wanes too soon,
The lilies depart,
And the flowers fair."

Night, and starlight:
Gloom of April, dark:
And sudden, hark!
The nightingale,
With mournful strain,
Piercing the silent air.
The Soul in despair,
Stricken with pain,
Echoes her wail.

Earth, and the sunrise,
And the morning hymn

Of the lark, when, dim,
He mounts in flight
The heavenly slope.
With him, my wandering Soul,
As the mists unroll,
Pinioned on hope,
Pass from the night.

THE HIGHER FAITH.

I set myself the task—O bitter rue—
   Which all the world since first-created man
Has wearied in the working—" Find the True;
Say what is life, and what our certain end;
   Solve the Creator's thought; define His plan!"

Through many years, through starry winter nights,
   In blushing woodlands warm with spring's embrace,
In summer bowers adorned with fair delights,
And autumn's quiet hours of ripened calm,
   I sought, and sought in vain, the unknown place

Where I might commune with my Soul, and know
   The close-locked mystery of heaven and hell:
And sometimes clouds would seem to break, and show
Wide fields of knowledge, only once again
   To close in night, and all my hopes dispel.

So was I thrown upon this antient creed,
   " I am but impotent to battle Fate;
God, in His keeping, has my greater need;
Why should I strive to force His will, and, foiled,
   Be cast in outer gloom disconsolate?"

Well do I know that, ere the Light of Dawn
  Broke o'er the earth, and rose the Morning Star
Of Promise, wiser minds than mine have drawn
The same conclusion, " This alone we know,
  Not How, or Whence, or Whither, but We Are."

Yet, though they ended here, or vaguely dreamed
  Of some dim after-world across the void,
Where the Elysian meadows faintly gleamed,
Lit by a Presence neither sun nor moon,
  And their belief on such fond dreaming buoyed ;

I, standing on the higher plane of years,
  At least am certain of another sphere,
Defined, indefinite, beyond all fears,
Beyond all comprehension, but assured
  As Death itself, that waits to lead us there

Another sphere, in which the perfect Truth
  Shall be revealed, and into wider scope
Of usefulness direct eternal youth.
So do I rest content, and, waiting, fix
  Unquestioning, upon this goal my hope.

MOONRISE ON THE GLACIERS OF
SAAS FÉE.

T HE holy festival of night ;
 The mountains awful, vast, disconsolate,
In homage at the great high-altar kneeling ;
The solemn flight
Of dim cloud angels ever upward stealing
Upon the snowy stairs, in fearful state,
Until they vanish, leaving but a star
Their footsteps in the trackless heaven to mark,
And point the way God bids my Soul aspire.
Listen ! afar,
From out the glacier cavern, cold and stark,
The wailing streams, that never tire,
Pour ceaselessly, as though the tears,
That Jesus wept o'er lost Jerusalem,
Must to all time for man's redemption flow.
Now, faintly peers
The moon among the shadowy pines, and, lo !
Upon the nearer hills, each towering stem
Looms out distinct, transfigured, glorified,

Knights of the Cross who, with their weapons bared,
Await the Great Commander's muster roll
In all the pride
Of chivalry.   So may I be prepared,
When He shall call away my Soul.

INTEGER VITÆ.

TO him, upon whose listening sense
  The call of birds at morning brings
An ecstasy of love, that springs
From wells of sympathy intense ;

Who, gazing on the summer sea,
  Hears, in the message of the wave,
  A cheering music, strong and brave
With hope of nobler things to be ;

Whose heart responsive treasures dear
  The joy of everything that breathes
  The procreant air, when hawthorn wreathes
The temple of the new-born year ;

In whom the anguish-stricken frame
  Of creatures, by misfortune torn,
  Wakes pitiful compassion, born
Of kindliness that knows no shame ;

To him is given what makes this life
  Worth living ; and to him is sent
  Fourfold the blessing of content ;
While, far removed from vulgar strife,

In a serener world apart,
He has his being ; and he moves
With the Elect, whom Nature loves
And dowers with her priceless heart.

THE COUNTRY LIFE.

A WAY from the tremor and blare
　　Of the close-thronged street,
The fever, the dust, and the glare,
　To the country sweet,

Where the delicate rosy light
　Of the setting sun
Pours through the latticed height
　Of branches dun;

Where the purpling elm bud swells,
　And the thrush, from his throne,
Clear as the vesper bells,
　Chants all alone

A psalm of infinite peace.
　O weary heart,
Thyself from care release.
　Silent, apart,

Listen, ponder, and learn
　The happy life.
What though we struggle to earn
　Riches in strife:

Yet, all the wealth of the earth,
    And the boundless deep,
Cannot buy careless mirth,
    And innocent sleep.

These are the heritage
    Of Nature's sons,
Heirs of a golden age,
    That ever runs.

Give me the country air,
    Far from the din
Of the hurrying thoroughfare,
    Where sordid sin,

And hollow laughter, sound
    Empty, and vain;
That, with contentment crowned,
    A wreath without stain,

Poor in the world's esteem,
    I may be blest
With the life I truly deem
    Sweetest, and best.

A FINE DAY IN FEBRUARY.

BORN, as a child out of time,
  Lovely spring day,
To be crowned with a garland of rhyme,
  And wither away.

Born, but to die : not in vain,
  For promise you bring
Of the glad incarnation again,
  The birth of the spring.

Even as a laughing face,
  Turning to smile
A moment ; a babe, full of grace,
  Waiting awhile,

With the wonder, and sunshine of youth
  Bright in its eyes ;
A glimpse of the infinite truth,
  That mocks our sighs ;

You have vanished, leaving us naught
  But the solace, and sense
Of a love that is lost, but has brought
  Love's recompense.

B

THE PROMISE OF SPRING.

C LEAR sky, and the song of birds on the wing ;
     The laughing voice of the brook, and the air
Fresh with the balmy breath of the spring ;
     The first, faint promise of April rare,

Borne in the music of bird, and stream,
     Wandering treble, and baritone ;
Love, for the flowing melodious theme,
     Love, and the joy of life, alone.

Are the eyes so blind, and the ear so dull,
     That there wakes in the heart no rapturous thrill
At the opening prelude, sweet, and full,
     Bird answering bird, river calling to rill,

Swelling the unison overture   -
     That heralds the bud, and the bloom of the year
The promise of God shall ever endure,
     Spring time and harvest—man need not fear.

A REVERIE.

I sit and dream before my pine-wood fire,
   The half-read novel fallen on my knees ;
A tiny flame curls out, whose glimmering spire
   Lights up her picture, waking memories.

Ten summers gone! Ah, me! how many roses
   Have spent their sweetness on the fleeting years ;
Hopeful they burgeoned, yet their fate discloses
   Love's bloom, and bud, ending in bitter tears.

Sunrise and sunset, shed o'er many lands ;
   Faces that smile, and echo fond good-bye ;
The yearning of the spring ; the outstretched hands
   That fain would clasp the shadows as they fly ;

Memories all—a tangle work of laces
   Upon the loom of life, by Fortune set :
For what ? To be forgotten, and their places
   Taken by sadness, and the long regret.

HEY, NONNY!

OVER the meads, with a bevy of showers,
   Spring passed, fairy-light,
And the print of her feet was jewelled with flowers,
   Scattered behind in her flight.

Whenever she laughed the birds replied
   From coppice, and lawn, and hedge,
And the stream, with long-drawn cadence, sighed
   His joy to the nodding sedge.

And, even as the wanton swallow dips,
   To the river's breast she flew ;
And, behold! where she touched her beautiful lips,
   The water-lilies grew.

Then over the hills, where the blushing west
   A bower of roses wove,
She swept away on her bridal quest
   To Summer, her Lord and Love.

IN MAY TIME.

THE woodland echoes with the song of birds;
  No hawthorn bush but holds its twittering
     choirs;
The lark, in ecstasy of wingèd words,
        To heaven aspires.

Gay are the meadows with the golden sheen
  Of buttercups, and, as he wantons by,
The cuckoo-flower invites with amorous een
        The butterfly.

The drifting apple-blossom sheds its balm
  Upon the orchard, making incense rare
Before the altar of the Spring, whose calm
        Reigns everywhere.

Sweet May that wooes old memories, as the flowers,
  To burgeon with the beauty of the past,
That bids our long-forgotten childhood hours
        Their cere-clothes cast.

What if your spell no present pleasure brings,
  No touch of loving hands, no trustful eyes
Gazing upon me; yet, your magic clings
      To memories.

This is a double anniversary.
  To-day the Love I cherished first took breath,
To-day my Love was torn away to be
      The bride of Death.

Yet, do I know that, as the roses wane,
  And have their resurrection, so, for me,
Through death my Love shall wake to live again
      Eternally.

THE LESSON OF THE ROSES.

THE roses fall ere summer time
   Has kissed away their blushes ;
The violets, in their dewy prime,
   Die ere the morning flushes.

The hyacinth, and crocus, fade
   Before the spring is over ;
The primrose in the grass is laid,
   Embalmed in fragrant clover.

The hedges that were hung with May,
   Are sered and brown to-morrow ;
The golden daffodils decay,
   And fill our hearts with sorrow.

And, through the woods, that yesterday
   With leafy ways were shady,
The north wind whistles on its way.
   The lesson learn, fair Lady,

That faded flower and fallen leaf
   Together are repeating,
How youth is but a season brief,
   And beauty ever fleeting.

A SPRING DITTY.

WANDERING by wood, and field,
   In the festal days of spring,
Where the scented poplars fling
Tasselled banners, lush with honey,
And the bees their golden money
Gather, with delicious humming,
Deep as distant sound of drumming ;
Wandering where the cowslips yield
Perfume light as maiden sighs,
And the purple violet spies
Through the leaves of yester year ;
What shall make us mournful, Dear ?
What shall whisper us of sadness
In this time of April gladness ?

Hark ! the air is full of sound,
Symphony of glad rejoicing,
Nature's resurrection voicing ;
Thrush, and blackbird's mellow note,
Nightingale with silver throat,
Linnet, laughing in the sheen

Of the elm-tree's misty green ;
Laughing, that his Love is found.
Spring to summer ; flower to fruiting ;
Linnet's laughter, blackbird's fluting,
Silent in short time must be.
Yet, what matter, Love, if we
Wander here to-day, together,
Through the emerald April weather ?

LES ROSES DE LA VIE.

IN the merry May time, when the lilacs bloom ;
  In the golden hay time ; in the summer gloom ;
Days of azure indolence : nights of starry silence.

Sweep of gloaming river, murmuring o'er the weir ;
Willow shades that quiver on the waters clear.
  Source of joy eternal ; passion ever vernal,

Love is hope undying.   In this world of ours,
Though our youth be flying, and the summer flowers
  Wither on the morrow, and pleasure turn to sor-
    row ;

Yet, while in the May time Spring her bounty rains,
And the moon 's at hay time, crown we, ere it wanes,
  The hours with love, and laughter.   Sad is the
    hereafter.

MOPING MUM.

A Merryman lay in the April grass :
    O, the sun was high, and the earth was fair !
And never a cloud o'er the sky did pass ;
    And his heart was light as the soft spring air.

The maid from her bower looked down on him.
    O, the sun was high, and the earth was fair !
Quoth he, " In life there's nothing that's grim
    If she smile on me.   Good-bye to care."
        And he sang aloud,
        For his heart was glad,
        The sunshine quaffed, and gaily laughed,
        " In life there's naught that is dark, and sad."

A Moper watched in the twilight gray :
    O, the sun was high in the heaven no more !
And the clouds rolled up at the end of the day ;
    His eyes were heavy, his heart was sore.

For the maid was gone ; her window dim.
    O, the sun was high in the heaven no more !

" What 's love," cried he, " but an April whim,
  As vain as the smile my lady wore ? "

   And his head he bowed,
   For sad was he,
   And " Alas," he sighed, " for the high noontide,
   And the light of a love that was not for me."

TO SOME ONE OF LONG AGO.

OH, she was like a violet,
   So dainty, and wee, and fair.
With the diamond dew her cheeks were wet,
   And the kiss of the morning air.

The sunshine lurked in each golden curl,
   And gleamed from her cloudless eyes,
And her voice was tender, and sweet, as the merle
   That flutes in the shrubberies.

The violet fades, the sunlight wanes,
   And the blackbird flies away,
But the sound of her voice in my heart remains,
   With the love of a by-gone day.

THE SISTER SPRINGS.

SMILES the Spring of the South,
    Smiles, and fleets away,
Holding her lips to the mouth,
    Where never a kiss may stay.

Flashing in emerald green,
    Jewelled with points of fire,
Anemone's scarlet sheen,
    Hot, as the South's desire.

Pleasure that fitful burns,
    Passionate love that is sped,
Or ever the hour-glass turns,
    And the April days are fled.

Comes the Spring of the North,
    Coy, as the heart of a maid ;
Scarce daring to venture forth,
    In her daffodil gown arrayed.

Blonde, as her sister is dark,
    Her sister southern-born,

With the voice of the morning lark,
  With the breast of the snowy thorn.

Whose cheek the livery wears
  Of the apple orchard gay,
Wet with the scented tears
  Of a weeping April day.

Whom to woo is delight,
  Long as the days are long,
Slow, in their stately flight,
  Beautiful, fresh, and strong.

THE TWILIGHT OF THE GODS.

THINK you the gods are dead?
  Nay, though in mortal shape
Blind eyes they may escape,
      They are not fled.

Think you the stress of years
  Withers the asphodel,
  And the Castalian well
      Has dried its tears?

Think you, because the dust
  Covers the shrines of gold,
  And in oblivion cold
      Old faiths are thrust,

Therefore their reign is o'er?
  Had we but vision clear
  Still might we find them here
      Just as of yore.

A MAID OF ATHENS.

L ITTLE you thought, dear Grecian maid,
 As you passed the poet's door,
That the charm of your eyes a spell had laid
 On the world for evermore.

You passed to the temple of Artemis, hung
 With jessamine, rose, and pansy;
But the snatch of the old-world song you sung
 Had fired Meleager's fancy.

While I, as the poet of yore, may dream,
 'Neath the oleander resting,
Lulled by the golden bees that stream,
 Their scented treasure questing.

Redolent was your honied hair
 Of the oleander's blossom;
Flushed with the pink of its petals fair
 The snows of your exquisite bosom.

And what though your life as the flower sped,
 And you entered the shadowy portal;

c

About your memory Love has shed
The glamour of spring immortal.

And, perchance, in the meads of asphodel,
You still sing sweet, and low,
Weaving the while of your fate you tell,
A wreath for the poet's brow.

THE BROKEN LYRE.

STRANGE that in summer time,
        When' all is prime,
My lyre is silent laid;
That, when the perfect hour
        Of fruit, and flower,
The year has made,
My music, that in spring time wantoned free,
Echoes no more with songs of Arcady.

But I am like the bird,
        Whose note was heard
When the pink hawthorn blushed,
Yet now is mute, nor sings
        His fond imaginings;
For grief has hushed
The rapture of the heart that found in May
A love, that was to last but for a day.

THE CALL OF THE FAIRIES.

THE Sirens are weaving their charms as of old,
   Where the blue waves beat on the sands of gold.
Sweet is their song : they are calling to me,
"Come to us, come to the beautiful sea."

The music of Dryads is borne through the trees,
As the leaves rustle soft in the murmuring breeze ;
And they whisper, "Come, enter our palaces, stay,
Where the forest is cool, and the summer elves play."

And, hark to the rippling lilt of the stream,
Where, white in the moonlight, the water fays gleam.
"Launch thy boat on the river. We'll waft thee away
To the land that's beyond the red sunset," they say.

But, clearest of all, there's a Spirit that calls
To the glimmering snows, and the stark frozen falls.
'Tis the voice of the Alps. Over hill, over hollow,
It echoes afar ; and I follow, I follow.

LONDON EMPTY.

YOU idlers stretched on the beach,
    Too lazy to reach
The pebbles you throw in the sea,
    " London is empty, who doubts it ? "
You murmur ; but listen to me.

Do you think that because to the north
    Belgravia streams forth,
And Kensington throngs the parade
    Of your watering places, that thus
The city in silence is laid ?

Do you think that because such as you,
    A thousand or two
Have escaped from the turmoil and roar,
    That London is mute, and your loss
The outer five millions deplore ?

What's summer to factory hands,
    What, fair foreign lands
And the sweep of the ocean divine ?
    They know not, nor ever may know,
What lies o'er the boundary line

'Twixt squalor and smoke, and the clime
  Of the sweet summer time.
Of the close-teeming workers, who toil
  For their hardly won wages of bread,
Ah ! how few may shake free from the coil

That winds them remorseless around,
  Fast, hopelessly bound
To the storm, and the struggle of life,
  Stern life, that endures not repose,
Breathing only of labour, and strife.

Have you, Master Fortunate, naught,
  E'en a pitiful thought
For the women, the children, the men,
  Who work whilst you play ? If you have,
Your rest shall be blest—only then.

SPINNING SONG.

SITTING, and blinking
  In the sun,
Dreaming and thinking
  Of days that are done ;
Sitting, and spinning ;
Life from the beginning
  Passing before me ;
  What may no more be ;
Flax that is spun.
  Distaff, and reel,
  Treadle, and wheel,
Turning, and turning,
Set the heart yearning
  For all that is gone.

O, for the spring time
  Of youth, and life !
O, for the ring time ;
  Maiden, and wife !
Age ever creeping ;
Waking to sleeping ;

So runs the tale.
All things must fail ;
Peace after strife.
Distaff, and reel,
Treadle, and wheel,
Turning, and turning,
Set the heart yearning,
Weary alone.

LOVE AND TIME.

SWEETHEART, the year is waning fast:
  The rose has fallen; autumn's ore
Tinsels the woodland, and the mast
  Drops from the beech's ripened store.

Upon the wind, a pageantry
  Of glimmering elves, the red leaves pass;
And jewels flash where apples lie,
  Among the velvet orchard grass.

Earth, like a weary child, would rest,
  Yet hesitates to put aside
Her sweet apparel, and divest
  Herself of all her summer pride:

And still, for you and me, displays
  A beauty even fairer grown,
Than when, down April's flowery ways,
  Love came in triumph to his throne.

Bloom follows bud; the stately fruits
  The plenitude of autumn crown;
So, true affection's attributes,
  By Time's advance, are perfect shown.

LOVE NEVER CAN FORGET.

THE winter fog, a nightmare grim,
    Upon the restless town is set,
The gas lamps quiver pale and dim ;
    How easy to forget.

I scarce can think so short a time
    Has flown, dear Love, since last we met
Beneath the sunnier southern clime ;
    How easy to forget.

The days of summer are a dream,
    The love they bore a fond regret ;
Their voices faint, and distant seem ;
    How easy to forget.

The mulberry has cast her gold,
    Tarnished is Autumn's coronet,
And dead the glory of the wold ;
    How easy to forget.

The rose to April's altar led, ·
    With bridal tears divinely wet,
Lies withered in her lonely bed ;
    How easy to forget.

Struck down by Winter's aching blast,
   She sleeps forlorn, forgotten ; yet,
So long as life, and hope, shall last,
      Love never can forget.

A DREAM OF DEATH.

DOWN the long avenue of gold
     With autumn fires a-kindle,
A Spirit broods, whose fingers hold
   A burnished spindle.
With thread of gossamers
     She sits and spins
     A misty shroud ;
     Chanting aloud,
     As the distaff thins
And the swift wheel whirrs :

" Here am I crowned the Angel of Death
   With the leaves the north wind showers,
As the woods bend low to my icy breath,
   And pale are the flowers.
For I weave the winding sheet
     Of Summer, and Youth ;
     Weeping alone
     O'er the days that are gone,
     And the pitiful ruth
Of the roses sweet.

THE FALL OF THE LEAF.

PALLID ghosts against the sky,
　　See, the wind-swept oak leaves fly
　Urged by winter's ruthless wand,
Hither, thither, helplessly.

To the earth they flutter fast,
Shrinking from the icy blast ;
　Hours that thrilled with rapture fond,
Phantoms of the summer past.

As the leaf, so must we fade,
Nor shall Youth's fair masquerade,
　With the happy spring time donned,
Age's wintry grasp evade.

TO THE ROBIN.

WHEN, in woodlands brown, and sere,
   Tired leaves are falling,
And, across the shadowy mere,
   Winter's voice is calling;
Sings the robin in the tree
Lays of tender memory.

Melancholy is the strain
   In the twilight heard.
While I listen, once again,
   In my heart are stirred
Fond regrets for happy hours,
Buried with the sweet spring flowers.

Gleams again the green arcade
   Where, in scented gloom,
April birds their music made,
   And the hawthorn bloom,
Showering light my head upon,
Gave me gentle benison.

All the glades to-day are mute,
   Sad, and desolate ;
Silent is the blackbird's flute ;
   Cuckoo to his mate
Cries no longer from the hill ;
Only you are faithful still.

Robin, who did blithely sing
   Anthems of delight
By the cradle of the Spring,
   Now, as falls the night,
Chant with me, beside his bier,
Requiem for the dying Year.

TO CHRYSANTHEMUMS.

WELCOME, blithe Chrysanthemums,
  Who, when drear December comes,
Burgeon into flowers fair,
And, with beauty debonair,
    Bring us consolation for
    Summer days that are no more.

Decked for Winter's bridal white,
Maids of honour, ye unite
In your robes of colour fine,
Russet-brown, faint opaline,
    Rosy-red, and glimmering gold,
    Such as autumn sunsets hold.

Gentle charmers of our grief,
In the falling of the leaf,
Breathing of the hours that were
Or yet the woods were bleak, and sere;
    Joy to all the world ye bring,
    With your gay apparelling.

UNDER THE LINDENS.

UPON the luscious linden bark
    I carved her name one day.
High in the heaven sang the lark,
    The world was blithe and gay.
For I was young, and she was fair,
And softer than the summer air
The words of love we whispered there,
        Beneath the linden tree.

December's dusk the heaven wears,
    And leafless is the lime
That weeps o'er me with dewy tears
    For the dead summer time.
All, all is changed.   My Love is gone;
The rose is sped; the dream is done.
Her name, and mine, remain alone
        Upon the linden tree.

"FONS BANDUSIÆ."

FOUNTAIN singing, upward winging
      From your lily bed,
Swiftly gushing, softly rushing,
      Lift your silver head.

Fountain, whisper crooning vesper,
      When the sun is low ;
Tune to slumbers light your numbers;
      Into dreamland flow.

Fountain, tinkle sweet, and sprinkle,
      Gleaming 'neath the moon,
On the flowers diamond showers;
      Morning breaks too soon.

Fountain, bubble, grief and trouble
      Come with dawn of day ;
Summer hours, summer flowers,
      Little time will stay.

A LARK SINGING AT SUNSET.

SOARS, with tireless wings,
    The lark to heaven,
Fearless, and strong,
In eddies of song :
        And I, in the silence of even,
List, while he sings
Of the innermost soul, and the secret of things.

Well do I love the sweet strain
        Falling in numbers,
From the azure aloft,
Tender, and soft
        As dew on a flower that slumbers ;
And, ever again,
Lost in the depth of the limitless main.

Yet, even as the heaven I scan,
        Fade on my senses
The song, and the lark ;
While the sunset grows dark,
        And darker the barrier that fences
The infinite plan,
And the wisdom of God, from the vision of man.

ROSE ASHES.

THESE be petals of the rose
    Gathered in an urn ;
Ashes of a summer dead,
Ashes of a passion fled,
    Knowing no return.

Seal them, ere their perfume goes,
    With a parting kiss.
They, that are so wan and sere,
Full of youth and beauty were,
    Ere they came to this.

And the lesson they disclose,
    Take it to your heart :
As the roses, all things die ;
Only lives their memory,
    As a Soul apart.

DREAM MUSIC.

THROUGH the dim Sleep City,
    In the grey land of dreams,
Echoes an elfin ditty,
Like the music of distant streams;
Gliding gently o'er the pebbles
With a laughing lilt of trebles,
Or, with deeper baritones,
As the water sweeps the stones.

So passes the elf song,
Dreamland's shadowy streets among,
Through the alleys, to the market,
Where, in wonderful array,
Fairy fruits are piled.   Now, hark! it
Fades in ripples far away,
Fades upon the senses ever,
Till the soft chords faintly sever,
And a single mellow note,
As of summer bees that throng
In a flower's velvet throat,
Trembles into silence long.

\

A FANCY.

Death is not annihilation; it is sleep. After the refreshment and rest of sleep through the ages, the Divine breath melts our slumber into life again, and the Soul blossoms as the rose tree in spring.

THE wonder and wealth of the East
    And the West are met to-night,
A nineteenth-century feast,
    A blaze of jewels and light;
But, under the spell of your starlike eyes,
The diamonds pale, and their lustre dies.

You spoke of the wandering Soul
    That, moving in rhythmic changes
Toward the final goal,
    Through countless æons ranges,
Ever, and always, upward drawn,
To be merged at last in the perfect dawn.

And I gazed on your face the while
    Framed in a glory of tresses,
And the full red lips that a smile
    Like a curling flame caresses;
And I saw the grace of an age long dead
Borne in the pose of your godlike head.

You, I should like to think,
  In the days ere the world was old,
Watched the drowsy tapers blink
  In some wave-washed temple of gold,
While the roses of Aphrodite fair
Mingled their breath with your maiden prayer,

As you touched her shrine with your lips,
  And prayed that no harm might fall
On the eagle-pinioned ships,
  That held your lover in thrall,
Far, far beyond the horizon dim,
Where the blue sky sinks to the ocean's brim.

And then to the lonely cape,
  Fragrant with purple thyme,
From your sisters you would escape,
  And the breezy headland climb;
Watching the tired sun to his rest,
And the sails fade out in the golden west.

Who knows but your life, dear Maid,
  Passed as the roses pass,
Which burgeon, glimmer, and fade,
  And fall in the autumn grass;
And, sleeping silent beneath the snow,
Wake again when the spring winds blow?

For this belief is mine—
    Death is forgetful sleep
That melts with the breath Divine
    To life from the ages deep ;
And perhaps I, too, in the days of yore,
Have gazed in your beautiful eyes before.

MONT ST. MICHEL.

THROUGH all the languorous hours of the night
    I watch upon these battlements to learn
If haply there be spirit forms and light,
    That to the ivied bastions return.

No sound of aught, save, far below, the seas
    That wail for ever on th' eternal stone,
And fragrant winds that murmur in the trees
    And through the crumbling turret softly moan.

Still summer night : above, the cloudless dome
    Spangled with myriad cresset-fires ; and pale
Upon the low horizon, trailing home,
    The virgin moon, wrapped in a misty veil.

Far to the east, and farther to the west,
    The white dunes fade in shadowy lines of sand ;
And vaporous wreaths upon the river rest,
    That whispers drowsy to the sleeping land.

Here, where of old was heard the shattering blast
    Of clarions crying loud in wild alarm,

And many a warrior's soul in anguish passed,
  To-night there is a holy, infinite calm,

Such as might wrap the cloistered monk, and nun,
  In meditation on these ramparts worn,
Muttering 'Ave,' when the day was done,
  Or 'Miserere' for a soul forlorn.

IN CHURCH.

SAINT Catherine in the window wears
 The crown of the virgin dead,
And the sun smites through the pane, and flares
 With a fire of gold on your head.

Pure little nineteenth-century Saint,
 I worship at your shrine,
For I know your soul is free of taint
 As the soul of Saint Catherine.

And, what though you wear no martyr's wreath
 For the sake of the faith, in my need
I pray the boon of your gentle breath
 For me to intercede.

AT SAN SEBASTIAN.

On the seaward slope of the citadel of San Sebastian are buried the officers and men who fell in the storming of that fortress by Wellington in 1813.

W HERE San Sebastian's citadel
    Keeps watch and ward beside the deep,
The sons of England, where they fell,
    Upon the bed of honour sleep;
The waves, their never-ending knell,

The flowery sod, their winding sheet.
    Brave hearts, that knew no mortal fear,
For Liberty such death were sweet,
    Though far from home and England dear,
Methinks, your resting place is meet.

For, sleeping thus, 'neath every sky
    Where Freedom breathes true life in men,
As sentinels, your comrades lie
    To point the way, to-day, as then,
For God and Fatherland to die.

POOR COURT.

*Among the graves at San Sebastian is one with the epitaph,
"Sacred to the memory of Poor Court, who fell under his colours at
the battle of Ayête, May 5, 1836. Beauty and friendship truly
mourn him."*

" SACRED to poor Court's memory,"
So runs the legend on the stone.
I know not, sure, whoe'er you be;
    I only know you lie alone
And look to England o'er the sea.

Beneath the colours, bravely borne
    Up yonder steep, Death clasped your hand.
Beauty and friendship truly mourn
    The leader of the gallant band,
Who sleeps within this grave forlorn.

SONS OF THE SEA.

NOW, once again, o'er the troubled main
    The winds discordant rise ;
From near and far, dark clouds of war
    Sweep through the stormy skies.

The breakers roar on the rock-bound shore
    Of the islands of the North ;
And Ocean proud, with a greeting loud,
    Shouts, as her sons go forth,

Loud and long, a glorious song,
    That nerves the arm of steel
With strength to shake the world, and break
    The pride of the foeman's keel.

And, wherever the guns of Britain's sons
    Salute the flag on high,
"Sons of the sea, be true to me,"
    The answering billows cry.

"Be true, for I hold the crown of gold
    Ye tore from the Frenchman's brow,

When rose the star of Trafalgar,
  And the power of Spain lay low.

" Be true to the past : keep sure, and fast,
  The empire of the sea,   .
Won by the might of antient right,
  For God and Liberty."

THE LOVER'S FAITH.

I N the poplars tall
The wind is crying:
The swallows are flying: ˊ
The brown leaves fall:
" Summer is dying,"
The robins call.

On the turrets grey
The Virginian creeper
Deeper and deeper
Blushes to-day,
Where Autumn, the Reaper,
Takes his way.

I sit beneath
The mantled tower,
Whose tendrils shower
To earth a wreath;
The blood-red dower,
And crown of Death.

Now in the west
    The sun sinks lower,
    And every flower,
By the dew oppressed,
    Bends to the Mower
Its drooping crest.

I too have known
    The spring time fleeting,
    And, in its sweeting,
The flower sown,
    And winter beating
On blossom strown.

Yet, though Death rend
    Flower, and fruiting,
    And birds be muting,
This faith I tend
    Past all disputing,
Love has no end.

A MESSAGE.

SUMMER breeze of the south,
　Swallow that northward dips,
Take this kiss from my mouth
　To my Lover's lips.

Whisper soft in her ear,
　As she watches beneath the moon,
Whisper, that none may hear,
　" Come to me soon.

"Come to me soon, o'er the sea,
　Lest I, as the flowers, wither,
And cold my kisses be,
　When thou comest hither."

MEMORIES.

THE laughing song of the linnet,
   A glade of twinkling wood ;
Each honied hour a minute.
  O ! but to live was good,
   With my hand in yours, and a flood
Of golden hair within it.

The blaze of the afternoon
   Out in the cornfields fair,
The vaporous drowsy swoon
   Of the summer landscape rare ;
   Only to watch with you there
To the rising of the moon.

The wail of the winter wind,
  Crying o'er moor, and wold,
That ever seeketh to find
   The heart that was mine of old.
   Ah, me ! for the love that is cold,
And the days when you were kind.

LOVE AND WAR.

THE scent of the roses, and night
  Watchful with many a star;
Two hearts with a single delight;
  The fortune of love, and of war.

The glory of battle; the beat
  Of the drum to the charge from afar;
Squadrons that thunder and meet;
  The fortune of love, and of war.

Roses, that winter and rain
  Blast with cold kisses, and scar;
Solitude, anger, and pain;
  The fortune of love, and of war.

Tempest of iron, and breath
  Of bullets that murder and mar;
Banners ensanguined with death;
  The fortune of love, and of war.

REGRETS.

THE gleam of a summer sea,
  The scent of a summer night ;
What can ye give to me
  Of a past and dead delight ?

Fluttering handkerchief
  Over the battlements gray ;
A fairy vision brief,
  That fades in the far away ;

April showers, shed
  From a heaven of azure eyes.
Ah, me ! for the love that is sped.
  Ah, me ! for the time that flies.

AUTUMN VIOLETS.

SWEET violet,
   The dews, that wet
Your pallid cheeks,
   Are tears of grief
   For summer brief,
And Love's defection.

But, with your scent,
A charm is blent,
That certain speaks
   Of springs to be,
   When I shall see
Love's resurrection.

ANNIVERSARY.

FIVE years! and each a link
   Thrid on a golden chain ;
And, O! to think
They ne'er may be again ;
Laughter, and love, and pain,
Beads of a rosary fair,
   Gems of a carcanet fine ;
Naught left, but the gray despair
   For a heart that might have been mine.

LOOKING BACK.

M Y Amélie, I've not forgot
 The pleasant garden at Handaye,
The sycamores, the seaward spot,
 That looks o'er Bidassoa bay.

Winter has torn with ruthless hands
 The trellised arbours, and the sea
Storms angry o'er the cold gray sands ;
 Yet, will it always be for me

A memory of wood, and stream,
 With winding paths among the trees,
Between whose latticed branches gleam
 The snow-capped towers of Pyrenees,

Where we, together, walked alone,
 Dear Heart, the magic summer night,
And kissed, and parted, when the moon
 Behind the mountains veiled her light.

Ah, fond farewell ! Ah, summer sweet !
 Though waves divide us, Amélie,
My thoughts go out on pinions fleet,
 And southward wing their way to thee.

TAMBINOK'S SONG.

Asked what his songs were about, Tambinok replied, "Sweethearts, and trees, and the sea."

R. L. STEVENSON, "VALIMA LETTERS."

" SWEETHEARTS, and trees, and the sea,
     These be the threads of my song,
  Woven bright fancies among:
  All that is dearest to me.

" Surely contentment were mine,
    Blest with the love of a maid,
    And lulled, 'neath the verdurous shade,
  By the music of ocean divine."

  King of the Fortunate Isles, ·
  What is more sweet than the smiles
  Of a maiden, a flowering tree,
  And the cadence of murmuring waves ?

  Sweet is the music that laves
  The silvery delicate sand ;
  Sweet is the long melody
  Of the wind blowing in to the land.

But sweeter the waves of her hair,
Sweeter than voice of the wind
The sound of her laughter, and blue
As the water 'neath tropical skies
The tremulous depths of her eyes.
Hail! Poet King, for you sing
All that is noble, and fair,
All that is tender, and true.

VALE.

L ET me but look into thine eyes,
    Forgetting all but thee.
Let me but touch thy lips with mine,
    In ecstasy.
The eyes, which are the index of thy soul,
    I would possess.
The lips, that breathe of love,
    I fain would press,

And, like a bird
    That skims the river,
Would take one kiss
    And part for ever ;
Or, as the bee
    That wooes the rose,
One moment sweet,
    And onward goes,
So would I kiss,
    And, kissing, sever.

PRÆTERITA.

I wandered in a garden fair,
  And plucked a rose that blossomed there ;
Passed, and forgot; the petals fell.
Ah! then I realised too well
The garden was the time of Youth,
And Love the snowy rose's ruth.

LULLABY.

SLEEP till the rosy day
  Shall chase away
    Night's indolence.
Alas! too soon
The silver moon
    Must cloak her radiance.
Forgetfulness of pain
In slumber lies ;
And weary eyes
But wake to weep again.

ADVICE TO YOUTH

THE shadow moves upon the dial,
   The rose-leaf petals fall;
Time will abide no maid's denial,
   Age waits alike for all.

The bridal flowers that spring adorn
   Will fade in winter snow,
And all their beauty be forlorn
   That is so smiling now.

So, while we may, let us be gay,
   Nor heed the sun's declining;
Tho' Time will take no maiden's nay,
And flowers have but a little stay,
      What use is our repining?

AN EPITAPH.

UPON her grave the daisies blow,
    And whisper sadly to the wind,
" Here lieth one who ne'er can know
    What sorrow she hath left behind."

THE RHYMER'S WISH.

BUILD me no marble tomb
    In the desolate dead-cities,
Where all is decay, and gloom,
    Where no one cares, or pities.

But lay me the sward beneath,
    With a fair white rose above me,
That, sleeping the sleep of death,
    I may dream that the flowers love me.

A PASTORAL.

What love of fame, what lust of gold tempted thee away from the red cliffs, and grey olives, and wells of black maidenhair?

ANDREW LANG, "LETTERS TO DEAD AUTHORS—
THEOCRITUS."

A PASTORAL.

I.

THE dust of worldly care lies deep
  Upon my lyre's golden strings;
Nor may my ears the harvest reap
  Of Nature's sweet imaginings.

I bartered love for worthless dross;
  My art made prostitute to earn
A wretched dole. And O, the loss
  Of that which never may return.

Have ye no word of comfort for
  My aching heart, ye woodlands fair?
Will ye repose your faith no more
  In one who withers with despair?

Because I turned from you aside,
  And listened to the tempter's guile;
Because your worship I denied,
  And bowed to gods of clay awhile;

F

Have ye no pity?   Shall the Spring,
   That once of promise whispered clear,
No message of forgiveness bring,
   No hope that love awaits me here?

The nightingale shall sing again,
   The kingcups shimmer in the light,
The snowy apple orchards rain
   Their perfume on the April night;

My ears may hear, my eyes may see,
   But spring shall only wake regret;
Nature, that smiled, and spoke to me,
   Upon her lips a seal has set.

Ah, me! that I should choose to spurn
   The talisman of heart's content:
How dear the rose, we only learn,
   When all its bravery is spent.

II.

I, like Theocritus of yore,
    Turned from the countryside,
Lured by the goblin store,
And the harlot pride,
Of the gaudy town;
Turned from the court
Of the forest green,
Deaf to the voice of the stream,
Sounding o'er fern-fringed pools;
Joined the army of fools
In a mad, gray dream,
And happiness sought
With the Great Unclean.

III.

SWEET Sicilian singer,
    Who cares for thy courtier song ?
Faint are the echoes that linger
    Upon the ages long
Of thine Alexandrian lays.
Nay, we have woven thy bays
    With pansies of Leontine
    And the tamarisk twine
To thy memory, green
    From the Taorminian steep,
    Where the blue waves weep
For the days that have been.

Where is thy great repute
    As lord of men, and affairs ?
    Who knows, or cares ?
We hear but the lute,
    Strung on Syracuse hills,
    Whose music fills
All time with Arcadian airs.

IV.

WAS the world fairer then?
　　Are we modern men,
And women, worse?
Or is it thy magic verse,
That, shrouding the past
In a glimmering veil,
O'er the old time cast,
Makes the life behind
Seem beautiful, kind
As a fairy tale?

V.

THOU, in the world's first dewy morn,
Singing, by meadow and down,
Music, sweet as the echoes blown
From the birds in the bridal thorn;
Whàt joy didst thou find in the din and the strife
Of the fitful fever that men call Life?

What were the women of fashion to thee,
With their white, inanimate faces?
Hadst thou not danced with the Graces
On the crocus-spangled lea,
Light as the clouds that hover and glide
With gossamer wings on the mountain side?

What were the musk and ambergris
To the violet's dewy chalice?
Where, in Ptolemy's palace,
Foundest thou lady's kiss
Soft as the breath the sea nymphs gave
To thy poet lips, from the summer wave?

VI.

SILENT my lyre for long,
  Nor sound, nor song
To cheer my way.
Come, where the shadows pass
Over the velvet grass,
And sunbeams play :
Come, where the lichens girth
The murmuring beeches :
Come, where dear mother Earth
Her wisdom teaches ;
Where the laughter and mirth
Of the spice smelling woodland
Strengthens the wings
And cleanses the strings
Of the dust-worn lyre :
Come to the good land
Of homestead, and byre,
Where the patient cows,
Driven from the meadow,
Stand to the pail in rows,
In the eastward shadow :

There shall be music here,
Far from the smoke-land dreary
Of city heat ;
Lute-string, and oat-pipe clear ;
Echoes to greet
The heart-weary.

VII.

So, I am back again,
  Back from the glistering heat
 Of the close-thronged street,
And the anger and pain
Of the struggling city.
Here, under the blue sky,
With the canopy
Of limitless blue above me,
Nature will pity,
And once more for her own,
As a prodigal son
Will take me and love me.

O, dear Mother,
What can the world
Of wealth unrolled
Give me so fair
As thy topaz air,
And the dew of thy kiss in the morn?
Is there another
Such glory unfurled
As the banner of gold
By the kingcups borne?

VIII.

IS this the same river
   I saw but yesterday,
Murky, and gray,
Sounding in gloom,
Ever, and ever,
Beneath the dim arches,
Funeral marches?

IX.

SPRUNG from the side of the hill
    Where, pearls in the haze,
The white flocks graze,
And the amber gorses burn
Like gems in the crown
Of the summer day;
With many a babbling rill,
And music of waters blown
Through briar and fern,
To the soft-bosomed vale
Thou speedest away,
Our own Father Thames,
Noblest of streams,
A god from of old.
Yet, not with gold,
But galingale,
And a wreath of roses, torn
From the midsummer thorn,
I bid thee hail.

X.

REST content with thy lot;
  Seek peace ere thy time be sped.
Here, where entereth not
The taint, and poison of ill,
Pause, and drink thy fill
  At the crystal fountain head.

Or, follow me to the end,
  And, following, be thou strong;
With many a curve, I bend,
Downward, and onward, borne
Through night to the perfect morn;
  And the way is weary and long.

Yet, in the end is peace,
  The infinite peace of the sea;
There from my toil I cease;
There, made pure again,
One with the ageless main,
Youth comes back to me.

Sweet is the honey of youth,
 And the green paths over the hill;
Here is the simple truth :—
Ever, with growing age,
The tempests gather, and rage,
 And bitter rains distil.

Because thou hast fallen down,
 And soiled thy knightly mail,
Still shalt thou rise. A crown
Of light by the peak is worn,
Whose slopes are lost forlorn
 In the depths of the misty vale.

XI.

S UCH goodly comfort did the River bring,
     To soothe me in my anguish, and, anon,
  Even as the snows that cloak the hillside, don
Their pinions, when the winds of April sing
To sleeping flowers the message of the spring,
     So passed my troubles, and, like balm upon
     My fevered spirit, fell oblivion
Of sordid quest, and empty wandering.

And, when the morning sun renewed the earth,
The evil dream had vanished, and again
I bade my lyre take up th' immortal strain
Of bird, and woodland, echoing loud the mirth
Of Nature's children, who with grateful sense
Fulfil the life of love and innocence.

THE LITTLE BOOK.

Princess, to you these rhymes I bring,
Children of Love's imagining;
But, should you scorn my trivial lays,
Forbear to damn them with faint praise.

IN PRAISE OF HERRICK.

YE gods who watch o'er Cynthia's fate and mine,
   Would ye but grant to me my heart's desire,
I would demand of you the strings divine
   That Herrick fashioned to his golden lyre.

So should my Cynthia live, though roses fade
   And beauty be as flowers of yester year,
A mortal love, by verse immortal made
   Without an equal in this age of fear,

This age when men are all afraid to speak
   The thoughts that passion to the heart dictates,
When, with false-sounding notes, and accents weak,
   Our modern love on cold discretion waits.

For me the goblet of red wine full brimmed,
   For me the burning praise of woman's eyes,
For me the song until the stars be dimmed,
   And morning larks take up our melodies.

G

This, this is life to warm the creeping blood,
  Resistless, brave, spurning the new-world sorrow
That neither dreads the bad, nor loves the good,
  That fares not laughing forth to meet the morrow.

Give me but Herrick's fire, and I will sing
  My love, my hate, my sympathy, my scorn,
Give me but half the strength of Herrick's wing,
  And I will soar on pinions heavenward borne.

BEAUTY IMMORTAL.

POET lovers, hurt of old
    By Cupid's arrows barbed with gold,
To the sound of tuneful verse
Would their pleasing pain rehearse.

Sweet and strong their voices are,
Echoing through the ages far,
And, like stars across the night,
Shine their Loves for ever bright.

Golden eyes, long dim and sere,
Rosy lips, that smiling were,
Maiden laughter, April rains,
All are gone.   But, yet, remains

Some faint essence of the past.
For, though summer roses fast
Wither, wane, and fade away,
Still, ere life be vanished, they

Softly o'er the china breathe,
And eternally bequeath
To the bowl their fragrant scent
As a lasting monument.

And, though youth and spring time fly,
Beauty's self shall never die,
By the poet verse enshrined
In the heart, and in the mind.

ST. VALENTINE.

COLD is our worship at thy shrine,
            Saint Valentine;
For, modern lovers scorn to heed
            The simple creed
    That swayed the mind of ages past,
And, at thy bidding, maidens fair
            No more repair
With happy swains, their fate to learn,
            Beside the urn
Wherein love's destiny is cast.

But endless quests of golden dross
            Our lives engross;
And though for us, with outstretched hands
            The sweet Spring stands
    Upon the threshold of the year,
Few are the hearts to whom she brings
            Imaginings
Of gentle love, to ban the cares
            Of base affairs
    That hold us bound in fetters drear.

Yet, while the love notes of the thrush
            Impetuous gush,
Thy matin song shall ne'er be mute,
            Nor destitute
Thy chantry of the hymn of praise.
Nor, while the bright-eyed celandine,
            With bashful mien,
Lifts to the bridegroom Sun's embrace
            Her virgin face,
Thy altar lack for votive bays.

THE SWEET O' THE YEAR.

TO pass the spring alone
          Were folly ;
Even as to groan
          For melancholy,
When all the world is young,
     Were to be most untrue.
     Ah ! when the skies are blue,
And broidered hawthorns blow,
          And dower
The grass below
          With many a shower
From boughs with snow-flowers hung,
Who would not happy be,
Roaming in Arcady ?

LOVE AND SPRING.

THE southward willow palm
  Has caught the sunlight fair,
And scatters golden balm
  Down the stream of the April air.

Over the emerald wheat
  The lark laughs up to the sky,
And the distant sheepcots bleat
  On the hillside merrily.

Listen ! the diligent bees
  Are murmuring at their toil;
There's a song in the woodland trees,
  A song in the teeming soil.

All the world is astir ;
  And smiles the green Earth good,
For spring has whispered to her
  The secret of motherhood.

O, for the pleasure of life,
　When the blackthorns blow again ;
When March winds cease their strife,
　And Winter forgets his pain.

O, for the perfume lush
　Of the dewy primrose flowers,
And the rosy, delicate flush
　Of scented almond showers.

Yet are these joys but fraught
　With sorrow, and Spring arrayed
With dole, for the heart untaught
　In the love of a man for a maid.

SPRING TIME IS HERE.

L IST to the ditty,
   Wise, if not witty,
I sing you, my Pretty;
   Spring time is here.

Soft winds are breathing,
Green buds unsheathing,
May bushes wreathing;
   Spring time is here.

Swallows returning
Set the heart burning;
Pity its yearning;
   Spring time is here.

Blue-eyed and bonny,
While it is sunny,
Gather we honey;
   Spring time is here.

April is fleeting.
" Come to me, Sweeting,"
Love is repeating;
   Spring time is here.

A SPRING VILLANELLE.

SWEET, to Love's music lend thine ear:
   All the world is young again.
Spring waits upon the threshold near.

Dead is Winter, cold, and drear,
   In a shroud of snowdrops lain:
Sweet, to Love's music lend thine ear.

Comes the Queen of all the year,
   Smiling through the April rain:
Spring waits upon the threshold near.

Hark! the thrushes, piping clear,
   Echo back the glad refrain:
Sweet, to Love's music lend thine ear.

Lay aside thy maiden fear.
   Love is sure a pleasant pain:
Spring waits upon the threshold near.

Wilt thou greet her with a tear,
   And with sighs that are in vain?
Sweet, to Love's music lend thine ear;
Spring waits upon the threshold near.

VILLANELLE.

KISS me, Sweet, ere April pass;
   The daffodils dance free:
Spring fades all too soon, alas!

The lark shall chant our wedding mass
   With rapturous melody:
Kiss me, Sweet, ere April pass.

Our couch shall be the velvet grass;
   Whitethorn our canopy:
Spring fades all too soon, alas!

The kingcup's wealth of shimmering brass
   Our festal bowls shall be:
Kiss me, Sweet, ere April pass.

Nor shall I want for hippocras;
   Thy lips enough for me:
Spring fades all too soon, alas!

Heed we, then, Time's hour-glass,
   Ebbing silently:
Kiss me, Sweet, ere April pass;
Spring fades all too soon, alas!

THE FIRST BUTTERFLY.

SEE, where she launches on her virgin flight,
   A pearl among the emerald of the trees,
Flaunting the pale-cheeked primroses,
Embodiment of spring, and spring's delight,
   The first, white, wandering butterfly.

So have I sometime wrapt in slumber found,
   Reflected in the mirror of my dreams,
   A form that through the vernal boskage gleams :
Greek Aphrodite whom the poets crowned
   Queen of their April Arcady.

And, yet again, one fairer still than she,
   Whose fearless eyes are clearer than the dawn,
   Whose soul is whiter than her snowy lawn ;
My English Love, that 's all the world to me,
   My Goddess, and my Empiry.

TO CYNTHIA.

THE violets bloom in the grass ;
  The spring winds murmur and pass ;
The birds are singing high mass ;
    Cynthia, come to me.

The bees are whispering low,
Where the scented cowslips blow ;
The waters sing as they flow :
    Cynthia, come to me.

For you the coppice teems ;
For you the primrose gleams ;
For you is the song of the streams :
    Cynthia, come to me.

But what is the pleasure of spring ?
What joy do the swallows bring ?
If, all alone, I sing :
    Cynthia, come to me.

MY LOVE UNKIND.

L OVE whispered in my ear,
  " Spring time is here,
The daffodils are gone,
  And yet, alone,
      You tarry.

" Is all the world so sad,
  Or, be you mad,
That, while there's hawthorn bloom,
  Such weight of gloom
      You carry ? "

" Nay, Love," I did reply,
  " 'T is not that I
Alone would wish to dwell
  In hermit cell,   .
      But marry.

Yet, is my Sweet unkind ;
  Nor can I find
Another maid her peer,
  With eyes so clear,
      And starry."

MY TRUE LOVE'S COMING.

THOU askest why my laughing lute
    So long was mute.
Summer was nigh; the woodland song
    Rose clear and strong;
The cuckoo cried, early and late,
    His wandering mate;
And to his bride the nightingale
    Told lover's tale.
Yet I alone, in doleful plight
    Wrapt day and night,
Sat all undone.

Thou askest why my lute I twine
    With eglantine,
And rosemary, in garlands gay,
    This happy day,
And why I fling aside my pain
    And tune again
Each golden string. Hark, in thine ear!
    Thy presence, Dear,
Hath changed my mood, and chased away
    The shadows gray
Of solitude.

ON THE SEASHORE.

O 'ER the gray dune,
   Where the silvery willows
Sway to the tune
   Of the tireless billows
Chanting all night
   The song of the sea,
My Love, my Delight,
   Is coming to me.

Spice-laden breeze
   Borne o'er the meadows,
Whispering trees,
   Under whose shadows
The fairies are dancing,
   Say if there be there
An elf, so entrancing,
   And gay, as my Fair ?

Winsome, and fleet,
   Through the long grasses,
With gossamer feet,
   My Lady Love passes.
Like a butterfly homing
   Among the white clover,
My Lady is coming ;
   Happy her Lover.

H

THE LOVER'S REVERIE.

AN idle hour, alone, to-night
    Beside the fire I'm sitting,
While o'er the wainscot phantoms light
    In shadowy troops are flitting,
And, on my contemplative eye,
Break scenes of happy memory.

Each spark becomes a spangled star,
    Hung over magic mountains ;
The jets of smoke recall from far
    The spires of misty fountains ;
And ashes white, that slip and fall,
Are snows upon the glacier wall.

Reclining in my easy chair,
    The fragrant herb supplies
Yet other recollections fair,
    As wreaths of incense rise ;
And, in the gloom, my briar teems
A wizard bowl of summer dreams.

The tendrils gray take form and shape,
  And, dowered with shadowy grace,
From out the wavering haze escape
  Faces that fade apace,
Even as my sense would closer hold
The phantoms of the fairy fold.

Yet, as the moon, unseen behind,
  Fringes a cloud with fire,
Making the outline clear defined,
  So, to my heart's desire,
Memory confirms the vapours faint
Into a vision of my Saint.

I see the curls that took the air,
  And wantoned o'er her brow
In little billowy waves of hair;
  Her lashes lifting slow,
Like pendant flowers, whose leaves embalm
The sparkling light of waters calm.

I see her head divinely set
  Upon her marble throat.
Her tender smiles, when last we met,
  Before my fancy float,
And gracious blessing pour upon
My lonely self-communion.

Until, at last, I know not how,
  Or if it be a dream,
My silent chamber seems to glow,
  Lit by a golden gleam.
And then I know, where'er she be,
My Lady gives her thoughts to me.

UPON CYNTHIA'S NECKLACE.

THESE pretty pearls were April tears
  Distilled from Cynthia's eyes,
Which, when they left those azure meres,
  Did falling crystallise.

Upon her bosom without flaw
  They gleam, and, thus, I know
That gentle charity will thaw
  The coldest heart of snow.

And those bright diamonds, that bind
  Her throat with sparkling light,
Are but the fancies of her mind
  Caught in their dainty flight.

Sweet are her tears, but sweeter yet,
  As sunshine after shower,
The smiles that Cynthia's eyes beget,
  And Cynthia's lips embower.

HER BRACELET.

THIS bracelet, on my Lady's arm,
 That once I gave to her,
Close guards my heart, as with a charm,
        Her prisoner.

And, for so long as she shall wear
 The band of precious stone,
So long my troth is hers, I swear,
        And hers alone.

And, should she from her wrist unbind
 These gyves, and set me free,
Yet would my heart such freedom find
        But slavery.

HER EAR-RINGS.

U PON my Lady's little ears
Twin diamonds brightly gleam ;
Like dew-drops, on white rose-buds laid
By tearful Night, they seem.
But, yet,
Are they more surely set,
Nor fade,
As does the dew at noon,
Which for a space its beauty wears,
Then passes all too soon.

Nay, they be guardian lamps whose fires
Attend the hallowed shrine
Where I have whispered holy vows,
And cherished hopes divine ;
And where,
Even as I raise my prayer,
There blows
A grace of frankincense
From her sweet being, that inspires
Love's noblest reverence.

HER PEARL NECKLACE.

A string of pearl surrounds her neck
    And nestles to her skin
Without a flaw, without a fleck,
    Transparent, delicate, and thin.

A rosary of marguerite
    To her fair bosom prest ;
But, not a bead of all so sweet
    As are the thoughts to them confest.

Or, are they tears that Cynthia shed,
    Returned to pearls again,
That o'er her cheek divinely sped,
    For sympathy of human pain ?

Since something of the Soul that rains
    In sunshine from her orbs,
This carcanet, methinks, retains
    And her divinity absorbs,

So that the very Holy Grail
    Were not more blest to me
Than is this emblem, white and pale,
    Of Cynthia's wondrous purity.

HER GOLDEN LOCKET.

THIS little golden heart
About your neck I tie,
And thus, with simple art,
My love exemplify.

For, as to your white breast
It nestles, so, my Sweet,
My heart would ever rest
In happiness complete.

Since, heaven were won in vain,
Had I not the reward
Of your dear love to gain,
And your dear love to guard.

HER RING.

A little thing
   This golden ring,
But all the world to me :
A circlet slight,
Yet holding tight
   A spacious empiry.

A pretty toy :
Yet all my joy
   In its circumference
My Cynthia holds,
And there enfolds
   Love's perfect recompense.

TO CYNTHIA'S ROSES.

YE sweetly smiling roses bound
    Upon my Cynthia's breast,
Ye, who a paradise have found,
      Be not so proud
      Since, thus caressed,
      Ye are but woo'd
        To your undoing.

For I, like you, did lately hold
    A place in Cynthia's heart,
And boasted, thus grown over-bold,
      My high estate;
      Yet, now, apart,
      Disconsolate,
        My pride am ruing.

MY LADY'S LOVE.

O dearest Love,
   Were the whole world beside,
The wealth, the fortune, and the pride
   Of great renown,
   My life to crown,
Naught should I deem
   The gain, if I
   Should lose thereby
Thy fair esteem.

Since, far above
   The height of such reward,
He that attains thy heart hath soared ;
   And dearer far
   Thy virtues are
Than all the worth
   Of treasures vain,
   That turn again
So soon to earth.

TO HER BLACK SATIN SHOE.

THIS dainty little satin shoe,
  Which hangs upon my study wall,
Was once a fairy barque—the crew
  Five elfin passengers, so small
That, when across the dews they went,
Scarce were the billowy grasses bent.

And in the hold for merchandise
  Were carried silks of divers hue,
White ivory, such as kings might prize,
  And marble, veined with softest blue :
My lady's foot, that has no peer
In either earthly hemisphere.

Ah ! happy little shoe that bore
  A burden light as thistle-down,
Here are you anchored evermore,
  Into a peaceful haven blown ;
And may this still your comfort be,
That you are honoured so by me.

For, through the seasons, I will wreathe
Your satin sides with fairest flowers,
Which, with their perfume sweet, shall breathe
Of summers gone, and scented hours,
When you, in all your pretty pride,
Upon my Lady's service plied.

MY LADY'S KISS.

THE rose's scent
        Is the embodiment
Of all the perfumed spring.
Yet, is her kiss
        Sweeter than this,
And hath no equalling.

MY LADY'S ATTRIBUTES.

HERA'S majesty divine,
    Purity of Artemis,
Wit of the immortal Nine,
    Hebe's grace, and add to this
Aphrodite's beauty rare,
    And gait of sweet Persephone
Yet, the whole may not compare
    With my Lady's entity.

TRIOLET.

YOU love me to-day :
    Will you love me for ever ?
Nay, come, Dear, what may,
It is something to say,
You love me to-day.
    Though hereafter we sever,
You love me to-day :
    Will you love me for ever ?

IN THE FIELDS.

A MONG the quaking-grass
          The blue spring butterflies
Flutter, and pass.
So have I seen
          My Lady's eyes,
Beneath their screen
          Of silken lashes,
Glimmering azure,
A priceless treasure.

And yonder buttercups
          That nod with laughter sunny,
As the bee sups
His banqueting
          Of liquid honey,
To memory bring
          The light that flashes,
In gold cascades,
From her scented braids.

MELISSA.

M Y Lady walks, with footsteps light,
　　Among the dewy grasses,
With webs of gossamer bedight,
　　Nor bends them, where she passes.

Her hair is honey-golden.　Brown
　　Her eyes, as, on the mountains,
The little streams that bicker down
　　The slope, in laughing fountains.

Her brow is whiter than the moon,
　　Upon the ocean dreaming.
Her cheeks are like the rose of June,
　　Among the lilies gleaming.

Her bosom is like hawthorn snow
　　Upon the scented hedges.
Her sighs, like summer winds that blow
　　Across the spicy sedges.

To flower, and stream, to earth, and air,
　　Men once their gods assigned ;
I worship her alone, and there
　　My whole pantheon find.

TO A BUTTERFLY IN LONDON.

WHY are you wandering here in town,
   White butterfly ?
Are the roses dead, the swallows flown,
   Is Autumn nigh ?
That through this dreary waste of streets
   You flutter by,
Seeking in vain for honied sweets
   In deserts dry ?

Cradled, perchance, with the poppies red
   Among the corn,
You woke to find your fragrant bed,
   Ere the breath of morn
Over the sleeping meadows blew,
   As by magic, borne
To this sad, strange forest of smoky hue
   And ways forlorn.

Or was it that Cynthia's face you thought
   Beyond compare,
And, even as I, by the glamour caught
   Of her sunny hair,
Followed her footsteps here afar
   · In fond despair,
Since the rest of the flowers as nothing are
   Beside my Fair ?

A GARLAND OF RHYMES.

TO my Lady's dear renown
    I weave these rhyméd posies,
Flowers in Love's garden grown :
    A bunch of summer roses ;
All ephemeral as they,
The fancies of an idle day.

Search the woodland, search the field,
    Cool, and pleasant places ;
Not a flower so fair they yield
    As her little face is ; '
Bee that in the bluebell dips
Finds no honey like her lips.

I the bee, and she the flower.
    Ah for summer madness !
Flits the bee, and fades the hour
    Into years of sadness ;
All that 's left a memory :
Bee and flower, she and I.

GAUDEAMUS IGITUR.

TURN again the hour-glass:
    The noontide sun hath sered the grass,
And the violets, alas !
    Burgeon, but to wither.

Roses bloom a little day :
Cometh age and winter gray :
Summer fleeteth fast away,
    And naught may call it hither.

Take the cup, then ; pour the wine ;
Let the rose our temples twine ;
Press thy dewy lips to mine ;
    Think not of to-morrow.

Spring her balm upon us showers :
Let us gather in the flowers,
Heedless of the coming hours,
    Bring they joy, or sorrow.

SONNETS.

MADONNA.

MEN crowned their poets in the days of old
　　With myrtle leaf and roses, while the fires
　Leapt, in their honour, into perfumed spires
On many a votive altar, wrought in gold.
What though the hearth, to-day, be dead and cold,
　The rose and myrtle choked by weeds and briars;
　Greater reward my every thought inspires,
And nobler ends my high ambition mould.
　For thou, the perfect mistress of my heart,
　My sun, the morning star of my delight,
　Hast lent thy presence to adorn my art,
　And gild my verses with a radiance bright;
　So that the blame is mine alone, if I,
　Through thee, attain not immortality.

MY LOVE'S RETURN.

L AST night I stood beside the sounding shore.
  " Wake all thy music; sweep the golden striigs,"
 The ocean whispered. " Borne upon scented wings,
Summer returns, and comes thy Love once more.
Far down the pathway of the moon, whose ore
 About the silvery-crested billow clings,
 The south wind wafts the homing sail that brings
Thy heart's delight." Even as the breezes bore
 The tidings onward, ceased the nightingale
 Her tender melancholy, while the rose
 Stirred in her sleep, and smiled, as one who dreams
 Her wedding hour is come. And as the beams
 Of morning drew o'er valley, field, and close,
 The herald lark took up the joyful tale.

MY LADY'S MIND.

M Y Lady's mind is like a garden fair,
   Fragrant with mignonette, and eglantine,
Pale virgin lilies, and the honied wine
Of roses, and carnations debonair.
No rank, unruly weeds may enter there,
   To choke the perfect bloom of thought divine;
   No poisonous canker creeps to undermine
The fruited buds, that soon shall harvest bear.
   Happy the heart that finds a pleasaunce free
   Within this garden of the Hesperides,
   Whence, as the petals from the orchard trees
   That gleam and flutter through the April night,
   My Lady's fancies softly take their flight,
   And fill the world with wondrous purity.

HER KISS.

THE hot clove-perfume of the love-sick may,
    Blood-red against the azure of the sky;
The fragrance of the lilac, swinging high
Censers of frankincense, in many a spray
Of virgin white; laburnums golden gay,
    Whose aromatic essences outvie
    The odorous gums of burning Araby;
Heliotrope, whispering of the southern day :
    All these I garnered in a posy; yet,
    Although the fairest scented blooms I wreathed,
    It was not till your lips of honey breathed
    Their long embrace that I perfection knew,
    And recognised my flowery carcanet
    Was nothing worth beside a kiss from you.

SPRING.

S PRING has put on her wedding veil of bloom,
    Of hawthorn white, and lacy guelder-rose,
  With chains of bright-eyed daisies from the close,
Where choirs of nightingales chant through the gloom.
Banners of welcome from the golden broom
    Flash o'er her path, as like a queen she goes,
    And, where the fiery-torched laburnum glows,
Musician bees with soft orchestrals boom.
    And thou, who art the embodiment of Spring,
    My little Love, with eyes of tenderest gray,
    And soft brown hair in which the sunbeams cling,
    While thou art with me, all the world is fair;
    Spring regent of the heart, spring everywhere;
    And life one long delicious holiday.

WOODSTOCK.

CALM at our feet the water's mirror-glass ;
   Above, an avenue of beechen green
Where shafts of latticed sunlight dance between
The curtseying leaves, and come and pass
In rippling bands.   The glorious morning mass
   Of blackbird answering, from his leafy screen,
   The lark—a present music yet unseen,
Far out across the velvet meadow grass.
   Thus to my fancy, like a silver dream,
   Comes back the memory of that happy day,
   Happiest, dear Heart, that you were by my side,
   When on the dappled woodland slope we lay,
   Watching the azure noontide gently stream
   Into the perfect peace of eventide.

ON THE RIVER.

SWEET is the deep and shadowy waterway,
   The mirrored avenue of stately reeds
   And scented rushes, where the moorhen breeds,
And drowsy ring-doves woo the summer day.
And sweet it is, in some sequestered bay,
   To watch the dimpling wave, while, o'er the meads,
   The distant chime our tired fancy leads
To lands of old romance, and lover's lay.
   Here do I love in indolence to dream
   The golden hours, and, with my pretty Saint,
   Whiter than is the lily in the stream,
   To build dim castles in the twilight faint,
   Peopled with fairy folk, whose elf-horns light
   Blow softly down the freshets of the night.

WITH A BUNCH OF ROSES.

THROUGH all the summer day my steps I bent
   By mead and garden-plot with flowers o'ergrown,
   To weave a garland that might fitly crown
Your sweet divinity.   The lilies, blent
With lush wood-violets, their fragrance spent
   Unheeded, disappointed, for I stooped me down
   To find the magic of their beauty flown,
Since I had kissed your lips, th' embodiment
   Of all that 's fair in garden, wood, and brake.
   Onward I passed.   But, ah ! 't was all in vain,
   And every flower but told the tale again
   That you were matchless.   Yet, for pity's sake,
   I plucked these roses.   Of your charity
   Accept them, Sweetheart ; leave them not to die.

A SEPTEMBER DAY.

A still September noon.   The sky in haze
   A glimmering vault of faint turquoise; the sea
  A soft expanse of blue; the melody
Of tiny waves, breaking upon the sense, a maze
Of rippling minors; shingle wastes ablaze
   With golden poppies' opiate alchemy;
   And inland, o'er the stretch of sweltering lea,
Pearl-studded downs where tinkling sheepfolds graze:
   And, at my side, a fluttering azure gown
   That billows close beside me where I sit;
   Two tender eyes, now grave, now laughing gay,
   A fairyland, where wandering fancies flit.
   Such are the memories with which I crown
   The sweet perfection of that summer day.

MY MEMORIES.

OCTOBER comes.   The shadows fall again ;
       The light of summer fades among the leaves :
   While I, half dreaming, view the gathered sheaves
Of memory, rich with store of golden grain :
Soft-scented beanfields, where the exultant strain
   Of morning larks answers the waking eaves ;
   Sunlight upon the fretted stream that cleaves
The emerald meadow grass where we have lain
   Beneath the hawthorn's broidered canopy,
   Watching the wanton butterflies at play ;
   Long shingle silences beside the sea,
   Where hornèd-poppies drowse the hours away :
   But, best of all my memory's garnered treasure,
   The love that made for me this world of pleasure.

FAREWELL TO SUMMER.

L OW in the hour-glass runs the silent sand ;
   Winter upon the threshold keeps his tryst,
  And chill November, with a shroud of mist,
Envelops all the lifeless forest land.
Here, by the grave of Summer sweet, I stand,
   As one who, bending o'er his dead, has kissed
   The upturned face, and, striving to resist
Fate's cold decree, clings to the icy hand.
   What we in pleasure sow we reap in tears,
   And joy is bitter in the after grain.
   Ah ! Summer, that for one short hour again
   I might recall thee from the bourne of years.
   Yet, o'er thy bed, I'll place no wreath of yew,
   But rosemary, that in thy garden grew.

K

LOVE'S CONSOLATION.

SWEETHEART, the year is waning to its close ;
    The wings of winter brood upon the land ;
  Bare are the woods where, wandering hand in hand,
We plucked from happy bowers the briar rose,
Fair emblem of the love that smiling grows
    Amid the thorns of life.   What though the band
    Of Months, compelled by Time's remorseless wand,
Like shadows flee across the waste of snows ;
    Kiss me again, and yet again, until
    Pinioned upon the wings of love I rise,
    And, as a soul that climbs the Olympian hill
    Wins at the last the gods' immortal prize
    Of everlasting peace, from care removed,
    So may I live for ever, being loved.

THE FAREWELL OF THE MONTHS.

DOWN the dim corridors of Time, to meet
    Forgotten memories, and disappear
  In the Elysian meads of yester year,
The'Months troop faintly, pausing yet to greet
My longing eyes, and smiling on me sweet :
  April, that whispered softly in my ear,
  " Awake, Love's resurrection hymn to hear ; "
May, that to thy dear presence led my feet
  Beneath the lilac bloom ; June, redolent
  Of summer roses, that in gyves of gold
  Fettered our hearts ; and sunburnt, glad July,
  That found us wandering 'neath an azure sky,
  And beckoned us within th' immortal fold,
  Wherein is perfect rest and pure content.

LOOKING FORWARD.

A year has flown, Princess, since first we met.
    Again the moon of daffodils is here,
And, chanting in the box-tree, loud and clear,
The blackbird charms away the vain regret
Of other days, and bids us, hopeful, set
    Our eyes towards the springtide of the year
    That comes again our longing hearts to cheer,
Crowned with anemone and violet.
    Sweet is the past and all its memories;
    The happy hours that we have roamed together
    By mead and down in April's magic weather;
    But, sweeter still, before us gleaming lies
    The road that leads to that fair Arcady
    Which Love, and Spring, have made for you, and
        me.

BY ST. MICHAEL'S.

A year ago. Ah, me! how time is fleeting,
  How quickly come and pass the happy hours,
Like fairy footprints lost on velvet flowers.
Well do I recollect, dear Heart, our meeting,
What time you came and gave me lover's greeting
  To symphony of music from the towers
  Of gray St. Michael's, with baptismal showers
Of linden bloom upon our faces beating.
  To-day, once more, those dreamy bells are ringing;
  Golden with wealth of bloom the perfumed limes;
  Delight to other hearts the bells are bringing,
  Nor thought of sadness echoes in their chimes.
  All is the same; and only changed am I,
  Whose Love is lost, to all eternity.

CHERWELL REVISITED.

ALAS! how many a spring has wooed the rose
   Since we together, Love, in Oxford were.
  Now, once again, I linger, musing here,
While, through the dark, the amorous south wind
    blows,
Warm with the breath of lily-plot, and close
  Of lilac, and laburnum.   Ah! how dear
  The memories that awaken as I hear
The nightingale fluting her tender woes
  Among the willows by the sweet, slow stream,
  Where, long ago, as in a silver dream,
  We floated, silent, listening to her song,
  Now faltering low, now rising clear and strong,
  Now fading o'er the water with her flight
  Far down the fragrant alleys of the night.

THE LONG REGRET.

SWEET autumn Violets ; the swallows fly,
   The sun is hidden in a pale eclipse,
The mournful rain from tired branches drips ;
Yet, do ye linger here thus lovingly.
Upon your cheeks the death-cold dewdrops lie,
   And faintly dies the perfume on your lips,
   Whence some belated bee an opiate sips
And sleeps embowered in dreamy ecstasy.
   Enchanted visions of a far-off spring,
   Dim woodland paths, red sunsets, and the gloom
Of starry nights, to memory ye bring ;
   And, sweeter than the breath of apple bloom,
   Your magic fragrance, falling on my sense,
   Awakes the long regret of innocence.

ON THE LINCOLNSHIRE COAST.

THE gray sea laps the desolate gray shore,
   Faint murmuring upon the sandy reef;
A soul forlorn, sounding an endless grief,
Beyond salvation, lost for evermore.
Against the sky, tinselled with golden ore,
   And garlanded with many a crimson leaf
   From sunset's crown of flowers, a moment brief,
A lonely sea-gull glimmers, borne before
   The outward wind, that with the soothing scent
   Of silver-leaved sea willow, marram-bent,
   And drowsy poppy, gathered in its flight,
   Hushes the troubled waters, while the Night,
   Stealing from out the west its last pale roses,
   Sea, wind, and sunset in her arms encloses.

VERSAILLES.

VERSAILLES; Le Petit Trianon. The hands
    That built; the royal lover: all are gone,
  And naught remains, but the recording stone,
Of all the pride of crown, and conquered lands.
And I, whose footsteps on the eternal sands
    Pass with the wind; I, wandering here alone,
    May muse, awhile, on love and passion flown;
The flowers of yesterday, whose withered bands
    Have lost their scent. For I have plucked the rose,
    To find, alas! how soon its beauty goes;
    To find new springs but wake to grief again,
    And summer joys pass as the summer rain,
    Leaving behind naught but the aching sense
    Of desolation without recompense.

THE NAMELESS LEGION.

TO you, the brave, the patient, nameless hosts
　　Who planted Britain's meteor flag sublime
Of old upon the blood-stained sands of time,
Shattering avengers of oppression's boasts;
Whether you rest within your virgin coasts,
　　Or where the tyrant, diademed with crime,
　　Watched, impotent, your stern battalions climb
The stair of freedom; to your glorious ghosts
　　Your sons, and grandsons, pour a grateful meed
　　Of praise, and thanks.　What though no marbled
　　　　cross,
　　Nor storied monument, your names recall;
　　England herself is witness of your loss,
　　And nations numberless, whom you have freed,
　　Stand of your fame the true memorial.

TO L. L.

A H, me! how many a rose since Omar sung
   Has given her sweetness to the wanton wind,
How many a spring time vanished, since behind
The veil he stepped, and from th' Eternal wrung
The Truth unfound philosophies among.
  Yet are green bays about his memory twined;
  For, though the Greater Truth he failed to find,
He brought men solace with his golden tongue.
  Here, in an alien land, remote, apart,
  Their old-time fragrance still those laurels keep.
  And thou, fair Lady, whose pure fingers sweep
  The chords of fancy, to responsive strings
  Hast tuned the poet's fond imaginings,
  Making them nobler, richer, by thine art.

IN THE NATIONAL GALLERY.

I wandered through the stately galleries,
  Musing an hour alone, yet not alone,
  For all the pictured life of ages gone
Was gazing on me from immortal eyes ;
And a Madonna, fair as April skies,
  Smiled as I knelt in spirit at her throne,
  Mute, with the ravished ecstasy of one
In whom all sense of other beauty dies.
  Then to myself I said, " Let her be crowned
  My heart's ideal, since, on mortal sight,
  Never shone vision of such pure delight,
  And none shall be revealed in time to be."
  Yet was I wrong, nor had perfection found,
  For, when I turned, I looked, my Heart, on thee.

RIVER RHYMES.

A MAY SONG.

SWEET, it is May again :
  O, let 's to play again.
Scent of the hay again
    Steals down the breeze ;

Flags are unfurling,
Whirligigs whirling,
Lilies uncurling ;
    Flies, how they teaze !

Bend to the oars, my Love ;
Never a pause, my Love ;
Cool are the shores, my Love,
    Wooing our rest.

Hark to the river song,
All the gay reeds among ;
Swiftly we glide along,
    Nearing our quest.

Here, 'neath the leafy screen,
Where the sun shafts between
Lattices fresh and green,
    Spread we our table :

Strawberries red and fine,
Summer incarnadine ;
Goblets of dewy wine,
    Pommery label.

So, while the ring-doves croon,
Rest we till afternoon
Sleeps, and the crescent moon
    Lifts o'er the beeches.

Then, since all joys must end,
Homeward our way we 'll wend,
Where the white moonbeams blend
    Down the long reaches.

Summer of joy, and youth :
What though it be the truth
Age follows fast, and ruth
    Comes to the roses,

Pluck we the flower. To-day
Laughter, and love, hold sway.
Sad are the hours, and gray,
    When summer closes.

ON THE RIVER.

'T IS the Month of fragrant hours
    That with sweet enchantment dowers
Evening twilight on the river,
When the poplars thrill and quiver,
And the night winds kiss the flowers.

Making music in the sedges
At the brimming river's edges,
    Moans the breeze beneath the starlight,
    While, a pale and dreamy far light,
Peers the moon above the hedges,

Flooding all the dewy grasses,
And the black, mysterious masses
    Of the twisted pollard willows,
    Silvering the tiny billows
Where the phantom driftweed passes.

Scent of melilot and clover
Wafted from the meadows over;
    Silence hushed, and only broken
    By the owl in covert oaken
And the ghost scream of the plover.

L

Fancy's faint ethereal essence
In our drowsy thought takes presence ;
  Form and feature gleam and glimmer
  On our sense, then, growing dimmer,
Fade and tremble into nescience.

Fade our fairyland expanses,
Snaps the chain of golden fancies ;
  Lights and opening locks awake us ;
  Back to earth their voices take us
From our dreamland of romances.

LEFT BEHIND.

BLITHE is the song of the scythe in the hay
                By the river all day ;
Sweet is the breath of the hyacinth rare
                In the soft summer air.
I will off to the river ; I cannot stay
                In the city drear.

The dust is white in the court below ;
                The pavements glow ;
The plane tree sighs for the gentle rain ;
                The sparrows complain.
What ! an hour yet before time to go ;
                'T is too much for the brain.

You idlers moored in the sedges green,
                Where the scent of the bean
Is borne from the fields on the whispering breeze ;
                Though the flies may teaze,
You are free to doze 'neath the leafy screen
                Of the willow trees.

The Law Reports are a thirsty task
    As I think of the cask
Brimming with cider, and iced champagne,
    In the lush grass lain ;
While you on the pleasant riverside bask,
    I must sigh in vain.

The gnats wind low.   I am half asleep.
    Dim phantasies creep
Into my slumber. A red sunshade ;
    A bewitching maid
With eyes of forget-me-not azure deep ;
    She trails her blade,

And leans on the cushions, and dips her hand ;
    By the breezes fanned,
Her tresses in gold confusion gleam,
    Like the sun i' the stream.
The boat glides on ; it touches the land—
    And I wake from my dream.

A JUNE DAY.

AN idle rhyme of an afternoon
    In summer time.   Where droop and swoon
The swaying reeds in the dancing heat,
And the shell-pink hawthorns bend to meet
The sleeping water ; I love to doze
And vaguely dream of winter snows.
Sweet is the scent of laburnum bloom
Wafted light through the flickering gloom
Of the willow shade, where my birch barque lies,
And the ousels wade, and the dragon-flies
Like points of fire glimmer and flash ;
And sweet is the garrulous water plash
Babbling over the weir a tune
Of summer and roses and leafy June.

A SUMMER IDYL.

A slow and weary local train;
　　An hour of sultry heat;
Then, to the river back again.
　　Oh! but to live is sweet.

The swallows hover, swoop, and splash,
　　And with the lilies play;
The little waves like diamonds flash,
　　And the scent of new-mown hay

Blows faintly from the upland mead
　　Across the flowery banks,
Where golden flag, and crested reed,
　　Marshal their stately ranks;

And, hung in delicate festoon,
　　Snow-white and shell-pink blent,
Dog-roses fill the afternoon
　　With summer's magic scent.

We 'll pull from Maidenhead, and up
　　To Marlow woods, dear Maid,
To spread our dainty feast, and sup
　　Beneath the beechen shade.

Then, homeward, through the mellow night,
    We 'll drift upon the tide,
Your hand in mine, your figure slight
    Close nestling to my side.

And when the silver moonbeams fall
    O'er river, mead, and grove,
We 'll sing a merry madrigal
    Of summer time and love.

ABOVE WINDSOR.

THE sun sets red o'er Boveney meads,
   With a primrose sky above,
The wind sobs softly in the reeds
   As I drift along with my Love.
Listen, dear Heart, to the river song:
" Life is short, but our love is long."

Over the distant wood the bells
   Faintly murmur and die,
Weaving around us fairy spells,
   Echoing dreamily.
Here, dear Love, in the sunset calm,
Join your voice to the evening psalm.

Over the water, sweet and low,
   Sing, as in days of old,
The lay of the humble maiden's woe,
   And Cophetua's crown of gold.
Were I a king, dear Love, I'd woo
Thy heart with a golden diadem too.

AUTUMN DAY ON THE RIVER.

A LL the hills are in mist, and the haze
  Creeps to the river's brim;
In the dewy meadows the cattle graze,
  Shadowy, gaunt, and dim.

The rising wind blows chill from the north,
  The fog-bank shivers and lifts;
Then, out of the clouds, the sun bursts forth
  And scatters the brooding drifts.

Like spectres thin o'er the fields they float,
  And, hark! the crisp, cool air
Is filled with the sound of the blackbird's note
  Chanting a matin prayer.

And, as our oars dip light along
  The glimmering waterway,
We too will crown with a garland of song
  The soft September day.

MAJOR AND MINOR.

West wind and east wind,
Summer and spring,
Fair wind and fitful,
Love on the wing.

OHÉ! the West Wind breathes
     Through the dreamy bowers of night;
The mist, in azure wreaths,
   From the river is taking flight;
And all the world is bright, and clear,
For you, and I, are together, Dear.
We have sealed our troth with a long, long kiss,
   The troth that is ours for ever,
We have lived our lives alone for this,
   And, with laughing voice, the river
Echoes the music of our love
To the listening moon and stars above.

Ohé! the East Wind blows,
   Black, and piercing shrill;
The angry river flows   .
   Dark by the storm-struck hill.
The wind will drop, and the tempest pass,
But I, and my Love, are gone, alas!

We have spoken the words of a long farewell,
　To meet no more again ;
We have wrecked our lives, and our love as well,
　And the sunshine, and the rain,
Never to us the same will be,
　For our love is lost through eternity.

DREAMING.

THE years pass by,
   The roses wane, and wither,
Old friendships die,
And naught may call them hither.
O, River, River, flowing to the sea,
Restore the heart that was so dear to me.

Sinking to rest,
The red sun floods and flushes
Thy tranquil breast.
Between the whispering rushes
My boat is drifting, idly, down the stream.
Here let me cease upon my oars, and dream.

Ah ! dear delight
Of youth, and summer weather ;
Through such a night
We floated on together ;
The moon, above us, pale as hawthorn bloom,
The west wind moaning in the scented gloom ;

Her hand in mine—
Soft touch for ever vanished;
Her voice divine—
Music for ever banished;
A coronal of daisies in her hair,
Forget-me-not, and roses debonair.

Fair garden-plot
O'erhung with leafy bowers,
Hast thou forgot
The Queen of all the flowers?
Tell me, ye Roses, happy by her made,
Where is my Love beneath the greensward laid?

Nay, 'tis in vain;
Poor tears are unavailing.
" Never again,"
The nightingale is wailing.
" Never again "—my Love is gone for ever.
Only thou always art the same, dear River!

AN APRIL MORNING.

IN Quarry woods the violet blows,
  The silver buds are breaking;
And at the river's brim there glows
  A fire of kingcups' making.
Come out, come out! The winter's gone;
The April sun ascends his throne.

The swallows round the ivied cliff
  Shrill out a merry greeting,
And many a pearly petal-skiff
  Upon the wave is fleeting.
Come out, come out! Our boat alone
Rocks idly by the mooring-stone.

And down the dimpled waterway,
  Round eyots fringed with willows,
With laughter light the breezes play,
  And chase the baby billows.
Come out, come out! The skies are blue,
And Spring but waits, my Love, for you.

TRIFLES.

IN THE TRAIN.

THROUGH tunnel's gloom,
  And cuttings gay
With golden broom,
  We speed away.

The day is fair,
  And Spring is sweet.
Away with care!
  Time's wings are fleet.

Beside me sits
  A girl of girls;
The sunlight flits
  Among her curls;

And o'er her cheek,
  Like wantons gay,
At hide-and-seek
  Her blushes play.

M

Spring's nameless charm
  The moment fills.
She means no harm,
  But kindness kills.

She smiles on me
  Like April sweet,
Bewitchingly ;
  Our glances meet.

A look—a sigh.
  Alas! I fear
It 's " Love, good-bye ;
  My station 's here."

SHE.

IN trim parterres the hyacinth
  And crocus gay are glowing,
The pigeons coo on frieze and plinth,
  The gentle winds are blowing ;
But, what though in her fairest gown
All London smiles, *She 's* not in Town.

Now Piccadilly 's filling fast
  With chariot, and hansom ;
The four-in-hand which just went past
  Has cost a prince's ransom ;
Yet, what care I for such renown
So long as *She* is not in Town ?

Though invitation cards may rain
  From Mayfair to Bayswater,
From all such pleasures I 'll refrain,
  Nor heed " Sir Georgius' " daughter.
Let maiden smile, and matron frown ;
They 're naught to me.   *She 's* not in Town.

At every corner flower-girls cry
  Their golden daffadillies,
Sweet violets on me they try
  And buttonholes of lilies ;
But, though they on their knees go down,
I 'll none of them. *She 's* not in Town.

Now glossy hat and well-built coat
  Assumes the Hyde Park stroller.
Let lounging hypercritics note
  The faded last year's '' bowler ''
Upon my head distracted thrown ;
I mind them not. *She 's* not in Town.

RETRO.

A summer night, a starlit way
  Among the briar roses.
A maiden fair, a lover gay,
  A kiss. Who now proposes ?

A wintry morning, sullen gray ;
  The roses dead and vanished.
How came it ? Nay, I cannot say ;
  But, alas ! for love is banished.

WITH A PAIR OF GLOVES.

THIS pair of gloves, white *gants de Suède,*
  Accept in payment of the debt
I owe you ; but I am afraid
  They 're not so white, Miss Margaret,
As are the hands they cover o'er ;
  So, lest I lose both bet and charms,
Just to the elbow, and no more,
  Wear them upon your snowy arms.

IN THE TEMPLE.

THE gardens are gay
In the Temple to-day
With flags, and the Horse Guards Blue.
But what do I care
For this flowery fair?
Strange blooms and varieties new
Are on show,
But I know
That the fairest of flowers are you.

The pavilion glows
With carnation, and rose,
Red lily, begonia rare;
But your hyacinth eyes
I award the first prize,
While the cherries are pale with despair
For the red
That is wed
To your lips and your cheeks debonair.

The band murmurs low
In musical woe
A valse, or a chanson of love ;
But the sound's hardly heard
When you whisper the word
That I long for, your little gray glove
In my hand,
As I stand
Bending down to your curls from above.

A SONG OF SCHEVENINGEN.

I doze within my basket chair,
    And muse on Fashion's folly,
Enjoy the sands, the salt sea air,
    And watch my dear Dutch Dolly,
With laughing eyes and flowing hair.
Alas! her beauty breeds despair
    And envious melancholy.

For, hapless fate! her curious tongue
    Completely I 've neglected.
Had I been diligent when young,
    And languages affected,
My mandoline I might have strung
In double Dutch, and to her sung
    The sonnet I 've projected.

" *Ik heb u lief* "—although the phrase
    Is hardly my invention—
I have unravelled from the maze
    Of Dutch verb and declension.
" *Ich liebe dich,* " the German says;
" *Je t'aime* " to maids of France conveys
    A similar intention;

" *Yo amo usted*," whispered low,
　　Will win a Señorita ;
Italians murmur "*Io t'amo ;* "
　　The Greek, in poet metre,
Sighs " *Zoe mou sas agapo ;*"
No words from Attic lips that flow
　　Sound to a maiden sweeter.

So, after all, if I can speak
　　Thus much in beauty's honour,
Be she fair German, Dutch, or Greek,
　　Française, or dark-eyed Donna,
She'll pardon my linguistics weak,
And, with a blush upon her cheek,
　　Accept my lays upon her.

AT COMO.

CLIPPITY-CLOP! The sandals ring
Over the cobbles, over the stones ;
Laughing and gay, the echoes bring
  Their musical monotones.

Clippity-clop ! Italian girls,
  Scarlet petticoats, nut-brown skin,
Swaying their fans, and swinging their curls,
  Pass the church within.

Clippity-clop ! A merry song.
  The bishop mumbles, the incense burns,
Chorister chants, and—alas ! 't is wrong—
  Sidelong glances turns.

Clippity-clop ! You are silent now.
  Maidens kneel in the mellow light ;
Organ murmurs Gregorian slow.
  Clippity-clop ! Good night !

HOMEWARD BOUND.

THE sky is gray, and dark the day;
 The autumn season has begun,
As homeward bound we take our way,
And bid farewell to summer sun.

Como and Maggiore gleam
 Like lapis-lazuli, and, gay
With vineyards golden-brown, the stream
 Of Rhineland wooes us yet to stay.

From wind-swept Alp and Norman shore,
 From quiet nook and sunny clime,
London compels her own, once more,
 To dingy office, smoke, and grime.

Shut up the Baedeker, and strap
 The gun-case, alpenstock, and creel;
Consign to shelves the tourist map,
 And swathe with care the shining " wheel."

The trees are withered, and the Square
 By Toms a howling desert made;
The Park is gloomy; gaunt and bare
 Are Rotten Row and Church Parade.

With ceaseless drip the rain comes down,
    On sodden streets the gas lamps shine;
But we must back again to Town,
    To work and play, to dance and dine.

THE MODERN GIRL.

A Modern Girl,
    With velvet eyes,
And a tiny curl
Of her dainty lips ;
To the finger-tips
Of delicate pearl,
Most worldly-wise ;
Yet a charming prize
    Is the Modern Girl.

A Modern Girl,
In a Paris gown,
With a creamy whirl
Of Venetian lace ;
Unless you can trace
The line of an Earl,
Or a million own,
You 'd best leave her alone,
    The Modern Girl.

A DISMAL DIRGE.

BACK again to the fog, and grime,
    The dingy skies, and the dusty Law;
Memories only the summer time,
    Sunny Switzerland, Scotland braw.

Back again to the ceaseless roar,
    The busy chambers, the stuffy Court;
The struggle of life made real once more,
    Existence a battle that must be fought.

But often yet in the long dark days,
    When the leaves of my lonely plane are shed,
I shall dream in the gloom of the mountain haze,
    And the bonnie moors where the grouse have bled

The white-walled castle, the distant hills
    Ablaze with bracken, the steel-blue loch
Whose rippling water with music fills
    The reedy bays where the mallards flock.

And when the wind moans in the chimney stack,
    And the angry rains on my window beat,
I 'll fancy me borne to Lochearnhead back,
    And the braes where the heather was deep and
        sweet.

AT DIVES:

A RECOLLECTION OF THE "HOSTELLERIE GUILLAUME LE CONQUERANT."

A N antient inn, as old, they vaunt,
       As the Field of the Cloth of Gold, with a sign
Of William the Conqueror, stark and gaunt,
    Wrought in metal of smithcraft fine.

A Norman homestead, rose-entwined
    With Gloire de Dijon and gay La France;
Portcullis gate, and a gallery, lined
    With paintings of women, song, and dance.

And, seated out in the courtyard gay,
    With earthen bowls upon their knees,
The dames of the Leremois-Marais
    Gossip, and shell the lush green peas,

Till the westering sun streams through the trees,
    And the sexton blackbird summons loud
To vespers the courtly congeries
    Of pigeons that over the gables crowd.

Then homely supper in Norman wise,
   Servant and guest, the same for all :
Flagons of cider, and great brown pies,
   Served in the kitchen dining hall ;

Lampreys dug from the sandy dune,
   Langouste fresh from the rocky pool ;
And a quiet pipe 'neath the stars of June,
   Smoked in the depths of the arbour cool.

Sleep on the eyelids gently falls ;
   Only the midnight bell awake ;
Peace till again the hen-roost calls,
   And the eaves at dawn their music make.

A summer holiday gone, alas !
   But still may its bygone joys respond,
Though the swallows fly and the roses pass,
   To the touch of Memory's magic wand.

THE DAYS OF LONG AGO.

IN golden days of Arcady,
          Long, long ago,
When kings were good, and people free,
          Ah! long ago,
A man might marry whom he would ;
This was a maxim understood,
And wedding bells, as e'er they should,
          With joy were always laden.

Then every maid was fair, they say.
          'T was long ago.
Knights never woo'd and rode away.
          Ah ! long ago.
And, strange but true, the fact I claim,
No fellow ever loved the same,
Or whispered jealously, "*Je t'aime,*"
          To other fellow's maiden.

Now, Arcady 's gone out of date
          Long, long ago.
We 've managed to improve the State,
          Ah ! long ago.

Each man who marries mates for gold,
And maids to millionaires are sold,
While on the altar flickers cold
  The flame of Love eternal.

But in the world's first happy spring—
  'T was long ago—
The beggar wedded with the king,
  Ah! long ago.
Love matches then were all the rage,
There was no need for caution sage,
Affection being the simple gauge
  Of youth and maiden vernal.

N

DONEC GRATUS ERAM.

WHEN Winifred upon me smiled,
    What happier heart than mine?
No other maid my love beguiled;
    None else I thought divine.

But when for me her fancy changed,
    And cold became her heart,
In search of other Fair I ranged,
    And vowed me glad to part.

First, Millicent the speedwell-eyed
    Close held me with her thrall;
Methought who in her service died
    The happiest knight of all.

Caught next in the embroidered net
    Of Sibyl's golden hair,
I sighed awhile, till Margaret
    Awakened my despair.

But soon as e'er my Winifred
    Repented her disdain,
I left them all, to be instead
    Her leal Love again.

WITH A POSY OF SPRING FLOWERS.

PRITHEE, pretty little Dancer,
    To my sighing give your answer;
"Woo me, if you think you can, Sir,"
    Seem to say your laughing eyes.

Atalanta tripped not fleeter,
Nor, with glances, challenged sweeter
Swift Hippomenes to meet her
    In the race, and win the prize.

Be my golden lure these posies,
Though, methinks, no flower that blows is
Half so radiant as the roses
    That your cheeks with blushes fill.

And your dainty hands are whiter
Than the lily; footsteps lighter
Than mimosa down; and slighter
    Your fair form than daffodil;

While, as nothing to the dower
That your perfumed lips embower
Is the scent of gillyflower,
    And of purple violet.

Yet, I bring you virgin lilies,
Violets, and daffadillies,
Feathery mimosa, gillies,
    In a flowery garland set.

Take them, Mistress, and remember
Droops the flame, and cools the ember ;
Spring will turn to bleak December ;
    Age accept no maiden nays.

And may I, as they, confessing
Earth has no more perfect blessing
Than my Lady's fond caressing,
    In your love rejoice always.

A PAIR OF SATIN SHOES.

hic paries habebit
lævum marinæ qui Veneris latus
custodit. hic, hic ponite lucida
funalia, et vectis, et arcus.

HORACE.

A S sailors won from stormy fate
To Aphrodite dedicate
A tiny ship of fashion rude
In token of their gratitude;
So, here, these pretty shoes for me
Proclaim my Lady's charity.

Ah! dainty little satin " threes,"
My Sweetheart's trim-built argosies,
That bore her well in crush, and ball,
Safe anchored on my study wall,
In peaceful haven you shall rest,
Of all my treasures, treasured best.

Her rosy feet and silken hose
It was your fortune to enclose:
How often in the mazy dance
You saw them twinkle, gleam, and glance!
E'en now, abandoned, serve you yet
To store cigar and cigarette.

Here Russian, and luxurious Turk,
With opiate Egyptian, lurk ;
Virginians too, a packet rare,
Soft as the southern summer air
With leaves of perfumed nicotine
Warmed by Havana's air divine.

And, as their incense faintly breathes,
And upward floats in azure wreaths,
A magic power I may invoke
From out the cloudy realms of smoke ;
And, in the haze 'tis mine to trace
The outline of my Lady's face.

LOVE À LA MODE.

DAN Cupid dons the wig and gown
  In this prosaic age of iron,
And *fin de siècle* maidens frown
  On love, and courtship, *à la* Byron.

For common-sense approves no more
  The simple ways, and fashions olden;
And, nowadays, by legal lore,
  Men to their promises are holden.

And gods who laughed at perjured vows,
  No longer flout affection slighted;
The modern maid a safeguard knows
  Superior to promise plighted.

For, won at last by fond address,
  All blushes, with a smile seraphic
She murmurs, "Ere I answer, Yes,
  Pray sign this contract lithographic."

And from the House of Somerset,
  By which, be sure, is many a fee meant,
Safe in her keeping she will get,
  Stamped, signed, and sealed, a tight agreement.

Then vainly strives the fickle youth
　To fight her with forensic fury ;
She has the bond to witness truth,
　And win her thousands from the jury.

LOST ILLUSIONS.

A neat little god, with a smug little face,
  Sat and smirked in an elegant shrine,
And a maiden drew near with a nice little grace,
  And an "Ave" melodious and fine.

Before him the candle-grease sputtered and stunk,
  Sham jewels his bosom bespangled,
And his health in a very small vintage was drunk
  By those who for patronage angled.

Rose garlands, and marigolds yellow, he wore
  Festooned from his neck to the ground;
He was fashioned in marble, behind and before,
  And widely revered and renowned.

In vain did the maid on the godlet impress
  The wrongs that her lover had done.
Though she prayed day and night she could get no
      redress;
  But he smiled, for he thought it was fun.

" Won't you hear, little image ? " she begged and im-
plored.

Then, tearing her offerings away,

Proh pudor ! she found that the god she adored

Had two nice little feet made of clay.

À MA PRINCESSE.

I was in the crowd;
   She was in her carriage;
Graciously she bowed
At the Royal Marriage:
         I was in the crowd.

Would I were a Prince;
I my throne would proffer
To that maiden *mince*
(That 's French, unfeeling scoffer):
         I was in the crowd.

Passed the happy pair,
Sounded drum and trumpet;
From my vision fair
I was forced to stump it:
         I was in the crowd.

Millions shouted loud,
Duke and Duchess greeting;
You were cold and proud:
O, but joy is fleeting:
         I was in the crowd.

Perhaps some day, my Dear,
They will cheer your bridal.
I shall feel, I fear,
Impulse suicidal :
      I, among the crowd.

But, whether maid or wife,
July and drear December,
I mean for all my life,
You I shall remember :
      I, crushed in the crowd.

TO MY LADY DANCING.

L IGHT as a rose-leaf, or silvery thistle-down,
　　Wandering on the faint zephyr forlorn,
Eddying, swaying, now hither, now thither, blown,
　　Ever on gossamer pinions borne,
Toying, coquetting, a dainty white butterfly,
　　Enters my Lady the maze of the dance
With a murmurous frou-frou as pretty skirts flutter
　　　　by,
　　And magic of footsteps that glimmer and glance
In intricate measures.　Not swifter the shuttle flies
　　Over the warp and the weft of the loom,
Onward and tireless, while her fair April eyes
　　Gleam like the stars in the midsummer gloom.
Cynthia, deftest of modern Terpsichores,
　　Nonchalant, matchless in grace and in bloom.

TO THE LADY CHINCHILLA.

DEAR Lady Chinchilla,
 I beg you accept,
If kindly you will, a
 Rhyme twister inept.

Were I Bobadilla,
 With riches a heap,
Instead of a villa
 Suburban, and cheap,

Dear Lady Chinchilla,
 I 'd make you an offer
Of a house that would fill a
 Whole Square, and a coffer

Of gems from Manilla
 (If gems there be there),
So, Lady Chinchilla,
 Be kind as you 're fair ;

Say " Yes." Do not kill a
 Poor bard, who would brave
E'en a rabid gorilla
 His Mistress to save.

And of gay potentilla
 A garland I 'll make,
My Lady Chinchilla,
 For the rhyme, and your sake.

IN TITIPU.

D EAR little maid of Japan,
   With chrysanthemum crowned,
Flicking a butterfly fan,
   Bewitchingly gowned;

Bee of the flower that sips
   Finds no delight
Like the bloom of your beautiful lips;
   Merry elves of the night

In their gossamer dances ne'er wing
   As light as your feet;
South winds, as your breath, never bring
   A fragrance so sweet;

Roses, that glimmer, and flush
   With loveliness rare,
Are pale to your cheeks as you blush;
   And your voice debonair
Bids the envious nightingale hush
   In silent despair.

THE END.

THESE are the idle fancies of a day,
    And serenades of nights long passed away,
Composed, collected, for the old sake's sake—
A poor excuse, yet all that I can make ;
The lyric children of a changing mood,
Half joy, half sorrow, turned in fashion rude ;
Lines to first love, a wilderness of rapture,
Moments, alas! no art may e'er recapture ;
Even as the eyes that woke my silent lyre
Shine dim and distant.   Yet, upon the pyre
Whereon, in memory, that love reposes,
I strew not yew, but leaves of summer roses.
And so, farewell.   In all that's written here
May naught be found unkind or insincere.

www.ingramcontent.com/pod-product-compliance
Lightning Source LLC
Chambersburg PA
CBHW030131030726
47498CB00007B/2646